What People Are Saying about Rob Stennett's Books

As showcased in *The Almost True Story of Ryan Fisher,* Rob Stennett writes hilarious, wacky, and intelligent satire. That brilliant skill continues in *The End Is Now* to such a degree that it's hard to believe this is only Stennett's second coming.

> **Matthew Paul Turner**, author of *Churched: One Kid's Journey Toward God Despite A Holy Mess*

* * *

If any genre needs a good satirist, it's end-of-the-world fiction. Good thing we have Rob Stennett. He's the Christopher Buckley of rapture reading.

> **Jason Boyett**, author of *Pocket Guide to the Apocalypse* and other Pocket Guide titles.

* * *

Rob Stennett makes the apocalypse fun! He has once again served up a brilliant dose of family dramedy. With equal parts humor, pathos, and artistry, Stennett deftly examines controversial dogma through the lens of family dysfunction. The satire ranges from subtle to sublime. It's the best kind of storytelling—keenly observed, wise, humane, insightful, sympathetic, and downright rapturous.

> **Michael Snyder**, author of *Return Policy*

Rob has a way of undermining your way of thinking without you knowing it. Like a thief in the night, his endearing characters and hilarious satire will disarm your defenses and rattle your traditions. By the time you realize Rob has more in mind than simple entertainment, it will be too late. Some difficult questions will be staring you in the face and you might as well wrestle with them until morning comes.

> **Glenn Packiam**, author of *Butterfly in Brazil* and *Secondhand Jesus*

* * *

Rob Stennett turns another interesting premise into an even more interesting story. A prophetic child, the promise of rapture, and the ensuing drama that unfolds tells a cautionary tale of what happens when, in hopes of a possible someday happening, we ignore the realities and possibilities of the present. A page turner most definitely!

> **Lisa Samson**, award-winning author of *Quaker Summer* and *The Passion of Mary-Margaret*

* * *

Rob Stennett is equal parts Tom Perrotta and Rob Bell. His book is a sharp — but also loving — satire of religion in America. In the words of his main character, it's funny as H-E double hockey sticks.

> **AJ Jacobs**, author of *The Year of Living Biblically*

* * *

I've just finished reading *The Almost True Story of Ryan Fisher.*
Wow! I'm an old cynical preacher so I laughed. But there is a
part of me that winced and even cried. This is a book about
lies and reality and about what's important and what isn't.
Rob Stennett has taken us on a fun journey to a scary place.

> **Stephen W. Brown**, professor, Reformed Theological
> Seminary, Orlando, and author and president, Key Life
> Network, Inc.

* * *

Reading *The Almost True Story of Ryan Fisher* was like literary déjà-vu — the distinct impression that I was reading a
story from great literature. That's because in some twisted
way, I was.... Fisher is filled with brilliant sarcastic wit,
mostly directed against the contemporary church, though in
a friendly, non-vindictive way.

> *Christianity Today*

HOMEMADE HAUNTING

A NOVEL

Also by Rob Stennett

The Almost True Story of Ryan Fisher

The End Is Now

HOMEMADE HAUNTING

A NOVEL

ROB STENNETT

AWARD-WINNING AUTHOR

ZONDERVAN®

ZONDERVAN.com/
AUTHORTRACKER
follow your favorite authors

ZONDERVAN

Homemade Haunting
Copyright © 2011 by Rob Stennett

This title is also available as a Zondervan ebook. Visit www.zondervan.com/ebooks.

This title is also available in a Zondervan audio edition. Visit www.zondervan.fm.

Requests for information should be addressed to:
Zondervan, *Grand Rapids, Michigan 49530*

Library of Congress Cataloging-in-Publication Data

Stennett, Rob, 1977 –
    Homemade haunting : a novel / Rob Stennett.
        p.   cm.
    ISBN 978-0-310-32192-7 (pbk.)
    1. Authors — Fiction. 2. Supernatural — Fiction. I. Title.
PS3619.T476477H66   2011
813'.6 — dc22   2010042220

Cover design: Curt Diepenhorst
Cover illustration: Erik Rose
Interior design: Beth Shagene

Printed in the United States of America

---

11 12 13 14 15 16 /DCI/ 21 20 19 18 17 16 15 14 13 12 11 10 9 8 7 6 5 4 3 2 1

For Sarah

Then the Lord rained down burning sulfur on Sodom and Gomorrah ... but Lot's wife looked back, and she became a pillar of salt.

Genesis 19:24, 26

The fiend in his own shape is less hideous than when he rages in the breast of man.

Nathaniel Hawthorne, *Young Goodman Brown*

God and Evil

I would have never followed this path all the way down to its inevitable conclusion if it weren't for two questions.

The first: Does God exist?

And the second side of that question is: Does Satan exist? Not that I thought about Satan very much. And as for God, early on I decided that I did not believe in him in any way, shape, or form. I wasn't a cynic. I believed that people had the ability to do unthinkably kind, generous, and heroic acts. I just didn't believe God had anything to do with them. God can't protect a family as their minivan sails through a crowded intersection, he can't influence the outcome of a football game by commanding an angel to flap his wings to cause a field goal to slice wide right, and he certainly can't convince a man standing on a bridge ready to take the final plunge that life was worth living after all. God couldn't do any of these things. Not because God was a jerk — he simply wasn't around.

I didn't arrive at this conclusion by reading Richard Dawkins and deciding belief in God is the reason there is so much war and poverty in the world. I didn't come to this conclusion by getting frustrated with inconsistencies between the Old and New Testaments. In fact, I wasn't even reading much besides *Charlotte's Web* back then. And it's not like E. B. White influenced me — a spider didn't appear and weave "God Is Dead" into its web.

But this journey did start when something uninvited came into my room. I was seven years old and it was a sunny afternoon, the type of day where I should have been outside playing baseball until dusk when supper was ready. Instead I was in my room surrounded by Legos because I wasn't very good at baseball. "Wasn't very good" is being kind — I was a train wreck. The first time I ever got a hit I ran to third base. Everyone was screaming "No!" but I assumed they just couldn't believe I'd actually hit the ball. I played left field, and when the baseball came at me, I curled my arms around my face like someone had just lobbed a grenade. After a while I decided my afternoon was best spent skipping the humiliation, so I spent my time alone reenacting medieval battles with Legos. When I was in my room my parents almost never interrupted me, and if they did I knew there was a problem. And on this day there wasn't just one parent; both Mom and Dad were there. Dad stepped foot into the room first and said, "Charlie, we need to talk."

I broke into a cold sweat. Whenever my parents said "We need to talk" it was because I'd done something wrong. They never said "We need to talk" and then spend the next hour discussing what a great job I was doing at school or how proud they were of me. "We need to talk" meant they'd gotten an angry phone call from a teacher or a principal, or one of the neighbors was upset about something I'd done. "He was peeing on my prize rosebushes, Sally," a mom of one of the neighbor kids would say. And then she'd add, "What is wrong with your son?"

In these "We need to talk" conversations I always had a perfectly reasonable explanation. "We were playing hide-and-go-seek and I really needed to go. And I thought it was good for plants. Aren't there a lot of nutrients in pee?"

Dad would say, "No, son, there aren't any nutrients in pee.* We didn't raise you to act like an animal. If you can't be civil then we won't let you play outside at all." After that I'd be grounded for two weeks.

But on that day it was different. I knew it was something serious, but their tone was gentle and soft. Something bad was about to happen. "I just got back from the doctor. He said I'm sick, honey," Mom told me. Then she started to cry. I felt like I wanted to cry too, but I didn't know exactly what was going on.

"Your mother has cancer. Do you know what cancer is?" my dad asked.

"Yes," I answered, even though this wasn't completely true. I knew there was such a thing as cancer; I knew *cancer* was a scary and serious word, but what it was exactly and how it worked was beyond me. My parents accepted my "yes"

---

*Come to find out, there are several nutrients in pee. There are large amounts of calcium, magnesium, and potassium. I found this out later when I was in college. I called and told my dad, and he just said, "Well, you can let your kids pee on the neighbors' rosebushes then."

because they didn't want to get into the specifics. Besides, they were as mystified as I was.

"They're going to give her treatment," Dad said. "And the treatment is going to work, but the medicine will make her tired. So we need you to be really good right now. Help around the house. Don't get into any trouble. We've all got to pull together to fight this. Okay, son?" Dad said.

The treatment did not make her better. It made her skin brittle, it made her lose her hair, it made her sit on the couch around the clock and watch soap operas. And I would sit at the other end of the couch and discuss the plots of *General Hospital* with her. She was too weak to get up and change the channel (back then, we could only imagine what it would be like to be one of those families who could afford a TV with a remote; we couldn't afford much of anything with all of her hospital bills stacking up) so my primary job for this portion of her life was to switch the TV from *General Hospital* to *Guiding Light* to *Days of Our Lives*.

Toward the end Dad told me, "It's looking bleak, son. We're going to need a miracle for her to make it now." My dad was raised Catholic so we started going to mass to pray for her. I remember going up to the front of the church and lighting a votive candle for Mom. I remember sitting and staring at that candle and imagining God way up in heaven looking down at us on earth. I pictured God using his X-ray vision to look inside the church and see my candle burning so brightly and profoundly that he would use his powers to heal my mother. I fully expected I would come home from church to find my mother completely healed. She would pick me up and kiss me over and over again and say, "I'm healed!" through her tears.

But every time I got home she'd still be lying on the couch—brittle and as close to death as ever—watching soap operas. We recorded soap operas over every VHS tape we owned so Mom could watch them day and night. We recorded *Guiding Light* over *The Twilight Zone*, *As the World Turns* over *Jaws*,* and *General Hospital* over season 2 of *Silver Spoons*.† Our lives were being taken over by bad dialogue and unbelievable plot twists. But they were all Mom wanted to watch. Game shows were too loud; sitcoms too silly; my horror shows were too scary. Mom found her only solace in affairs and mistaken identities and confessions of secret desire.

Mom watched soap operas (it got to where she almost never left the couch) while Dad and I went to church to light candles and pray for her. And there was one night when I looked at all the lit candles and wondered how many of those were for other moms who were dying of cancer. Why didn't we hear good stories of things happening with these candles? Why was it the same people every Saturday night, the same hopeless stares, the same candles flickering pointlessly?

When we got home Mom wasn't there. We learned later she'd called a neighbor who took her to the hospital. By the time Dad and I arrived a doctor was waiting to meet us. He asked to talk to Dad in private, and through the glass in the

---

*Even at a young age I loved horror movies. They take you to another world and always make me jump a little. All my friends got a thrill from riding roller coasters. We never had the money for amusement parks so I had to find thrills from werewolves and axe murders.

†I didn't just like horror. I also appreciated the acting talent of Ricky Schroder.

other room I saw Dad cry for the first and only time in my life. He was still strong as my dad always was; he locked eyes with the doctor and nodded as the doctor was no doubt giving him the details of my mother's death. For a moment Dad looked away from the doctor and caught eyes with me. His look told me everything. It said, *Well, it's just you and me now, Charlie.*

When he finally came out of the glass room Dad wasn't crying anymore. He knew it was his time to be strong as he told me, "Charlie, your mother isn't with us anymore."

I was crying now. I asked, "Can we see her?"

"Sure," Dad said.

When I looked at her, I thought of the bouquet of helium balloons I'd gotten for my birthday that year. At the party they were colorful and full of air. They seemed ready to race to the sky—if only the ceiling weren't in the way. But slowly, over the next two weeks, the life started to leak out of them. At first I noticed they were no longer reaching the ceiling, then it seemed like just staying off the floor was a chore. Finally they were lying on the ground, flat and lifeless, and I could barely remember when they were so vibrant and full of life.

My mother was a helium balloon.

Life had been leaking out of her ever since that day she and Dad told me she was sick. Maybe that's why seeing her there pale and dead wasn't all that much of a shock. I did think about the last thing I said to her, which was, "I think Dr. White is secretly in love with Susan Ward."

We had been discussing the latest *General Hospital.* I was the only one around for Mom to discuss soap opera plots

18

with. I loved those discussions because Mom didn't look at me like a child. I was a peer and a friend. I think this change happened when she started realizing her fate. She understood she'd never get to see me holding a college diploma, she'd never help me think of creative ways to propose marriage, nor would she give me advice on how to raise my own kids. The most adult moments she'd ever get to have with me involved the plots of *As the World Turns*.

When we went back to mass for the funeral I stared at those candles again. As everyone bowed their heads to pray I held my head up because I knew there was no God to pray to—if he was out there he would have healed my mother. He would have done something for me and for all those other people who light candles and cry out for him to save them.

The pallbearers carried my mother's casket, and I followed it and left the church.

Any chance I had at having faith in God left with me.

2

Moving Day

For the next thirty years I did not seriously wrestle with any questions about God, Satan, the paranormal, and/or supernatural. But those questions started to reappear in my life shortly after we moved into the house at 1282 Voorhees Lane. Of course when we first moved I wasn't thinking about anything particularly existential or philosophical; I just hoped the plumbing worked.

Rachel tried to put a good face on the house. She said, "It really isn't that bad" as she pulled a stack of plates wrapped in newspaper out of a box marked "Kitchen." The sunlight shining through the sliding glass door made her hair glow like fire. She'd aged like a bottle of fine cabernet. Not that I was a wine connoisseur. I wouldn't know what a bottle of fine cabernet should taste like. What I did know was that Rachel was gorgeous as ever and I was lucky to be married to this woman for the last thirteen years. And she followed me here. To this place. Our new home.

She was being kind. She was trying to put some sort of optimistic, glass-is-half-full—

(Full of what, I'm not sure, but at least it's half full)

—face on this whole situation. The truth was this place was run down. It wasn't a pit. It wasn't like the front door shook when I sneezed. But it was half the size of our old house. And I'd moved us here so I could chase a dream.

I walked outside and saw Adam pulling a box out of the moving truck. Adam had brown hair, strong cheekbones, and freckles. The girls were going to love him. Actually, I hoped they hadn't started loving him yet. But he was a good-looking kid; he actually got a lot of his looks from his mother. Rachel hated that he had her freckles. It never bothered Adam. Actually, not a lot bothered my son. Not even moving. There was a bounce to his step as he carried the box inside. Moving meant new people and new places to explore. He could start over at a new school. Maybe this time around he'd be the school jock or rock star.

"Where does this go, Dad?" Adam asked.

I looked at the box marked "Living Room." We borrowed these boxes because we didn't have money to buy new ones— we didn't have money for much of anything. The previous owner marked this box and only Rachel knew where it actually went, so I said, "Better ask your mom."

"Sure, Dad," Adam said and ran inside. "I love this place, Dad!"

"Me too," I answered and wished I meant it. What I'd give to have the optimism of an eight-year-old. I tried to find some as I stood next to the truck and drank in the sight of our new home. The front lawn was completely dead; there weren't even dandelions or weeds growing in the soil. It was like the previous owners had watered it with arsenic. The whole neighborhood seemed like it was dying. Its heyday was probably around the mid 1980s. I could picture what the neighborhood would have looked like back then: women in shoulder pads driving to work and men in bathrobes grabbing newspapers with Ronald Reagan on the front page. I could almost smell the exhaust fumes of a Corvette down the block as some blond guy with a mullet and an electric blue tank top worked on it while Van Halen blared on his boom box. That young guy with the mullet was probably now balding and that businesswoman nearing retirement.

(You don't have to stay here forever, just until you finish.)

I grabbed another box, walked inside, went to the living room, and placed the box on the couch. I looked at the wood-paneled walls. It was hard for me to imagine wood paneling ever being fashionable. After this house was built, did some young wife turn to her husband and say, "Oh, Lance, this is perfect! I LOVE the wood paneling in the living room. It'll feel like we're watching *The Golden Girls* in our very own sauna!"

The kitchen was better, but the countertops didn't have nice tile with a colorful backsplash like our old kitchen did; this was cheap white laminate with weird shapes everywhere. The den had shag carpet with a nice mildew scent.

I went in the kitchen and Rachel cracked open a new box and put silverware in a drawer — the drawer I'd be directed to for the next few weeks whenever I asked Rachel where we kept the spoons. Rachel already knew where everything went, but it would take me at least a month to understand the layout of our new kitchen. Lucy was helping Rachel sort through the forks, knives, and spoons. It was great that my daughter wanted to help, but I think Lucy really just wanted to have a say in where everything went.

The move may have been hardest for her. She cried when I told her we were moving school districts so she'd have to make new friends in the first grade. The new house we found (at a price too good to pass up) was in Castle Rock,* about forty minutes from our old home in Boulder. We were close enough to stay in touch on the weekends, but for the most part my wife and kids had to make new friends. This was especially hard on Lucy. She'd gotten popular in kindergarten. Now she had to start over. Organizing the kitchen was her way of coping with the move, a small way she could assert control on shaping our new life. It was her version of building Lego castles.

I wrapped my arms around Rachel and asked, "How are you feeling?"

"Good," she smiled. But it was a smile that said, *Oh please, God, let everything be okay.*

* * *

Her smile had changed in the last month.

At first it was the smile of a fearless woman who wasn't afraid of anything. Back then she thought all of this was a good idea. The first time she ever heard my plan was at my birthday dinner. Rachel and I were celebrating like we always

---

*No, not Stephen King's fictional Castle Rock. There are no rabid Saint Bernards or shops where you can get whatever you want for the price of your soul in this story.

did, downtown at the Black Olive. I wore my navy blue suit and she wore her red dress with pearls. Dressing up for a birthday dinner should have made us feel special, but I think it reminded us that this was something we could only afford to do every six months.

"You still haven't told me what you want for your birthday," Rachel said after our plates were cleared.

"You don't have to get me anything. This is perfect," I said.

"No, I want to get you something. But it's hard to know what to shop for after being together for thirteen years. If you could have anything in the world, what would you want?"

I'd want to be able to finish my horror novel. But Rachel wasn't a genie — she wasn't offering to grant one wish. She was just asking what sort of gift she could get me. My problem was I didn't want golf clubs or a trip to Hawaii or anything else she or anyone else could buy. What I wanted was time to work on my book.

On New Year's Eve the year before I held a plastic glass of champagne and promised myself I'd finish a novel. I made good on that promise. I bought a laptop and I worked on it whenever I could. I thought up ideas for scenes on the way to and from school every morning; I jotted character ideas on napkins; I drank lots of black coffee to keep me awake whenever I had the inspiration to write. I wanted writing to get my best creativity and energy, but there were just too many other things in the way. Adam's soccer games, grading book reports, Lucy's piano recital, lesson planning for our *Lord of the Flies* unit, date night with Rachel, and sponsoring the debate team. Between all of that I could only work on the novel on those rare weeknights or Saturdays when I could sneak away.

Despite the challenges, I made good on my resolution and finished my novel. Then I sent the manuscript off and waited for the offers to pour in. The lack of time that I'd put into the book showed in the rejection letters I got from publishers and agents.

"Story needs more tension."

"Stakes need to be raised."

"Is this supposed to be a horror novel?"

"Not frightening enough."

"Not scary enough."

"Not interested."

"You call that a body count?"

And that's why when Rachel asked what I wanted for my birthday I just blurted out, "I want six months."

"Six months?"

"I want to quit my job for six months."

The waiter came and put our bananas foster on the table and lit it on fire. I must have looked particularly evil under the glow of that flaming dessert. "Wow, um, I was expecting you to say new golf clubs. You're a teacher, you can't just quit your job."

"Yeah, no, I should have said golf clubs. I'm sorry. I don't know what I'm saying."

"No, tell me. Why do you want to quit teaching for six months?"

"I want to write a novel."

"You've already written a novel."

"It's not any good."

"It's pretty good," she said.

"Pretty good. It can't be pretty good. It's horror. It shouldn't be pretty at all."

"You know that's not what I meant by 'pretty.'"

"I also know I need this novel to be great."

"Maybe it is great, Charlie," she said. "Honestly, I wasn't able to give it as much attention as I wanted to. I was trying to read it when Lucy needed me to hem her dress and Adam was asking if he could try out for the football team."

"He wants to try out for football? He's eight."

"I guess they have football teams for eight-year-olds," Rachel said.

"This is my point. If you don't have time to even read a book, how am I supposed to write one? Rachel, if I'm ever going to do something actually worthwhile, I have to have time. I'm teaching high school English and that takes more time than any other subject. There's grading, lesson planning, and I have to read so many papers and book reports. I just don't have the energy to do all of that and write a great story too. I had an agent contact me and say he thought I had a good novel in me. I can create that novel, but not out of thin air. I need time. I need all of us to make a sacrifice. I love our family. But I'd love to support our family by writing."

"Charlie, you're the one who said it's really hard to make a living writing."

"And I'm right. I'd be an idiot to quit my job to write a book. But I still want to try. I don't know what will happen.

Maybe my novel will really take off and be a bestseller. Maybe I'll write part-time and teach part-time. Maybe it'll flop and go straight to the bargain racks. I can live with any of that. I'm not asking for the chance to write a bestseller; I'm just asking for the time to write a novel. I want to write something I can actually be proud of."

"You're getting really passionate all of a sudden," Rachel said.

"I know. I think I really need this."

"You've been thinking about it a long time," Rachel said.

"Yeah, I guess I have. But I wasn't planning on bringing it up tonight. It's just, you asked me what I wanted, and if I'm really honest, this is what I want."

"Are you sure?"

"Yeah, I'm sure."

"Six months?" she asked.

"Six months," I said.

She smiled that brave smile. The one that said I'll follow you anywhere. The smile that said life is one great adventure and I'm up for the challenge. But all she said was, "Okay."

"Okay," I said. I couldn't believe it. I didn't plan on making my case that strongly, and I didn't plan on her going along with it so easily.

"All right then, let's figure it out," Rachel echoed. Her eyes were bright with the hope of the future.

* * *

Figuring it out meant selling our house and moving into a place with affordable rent. By fate, we stumbled upon this rental home. I told our realtor what we were looking for and our price range. He said we were crazy. Eventually he found a place all the way down in Castle Rock. The owner wanted to get someone in as quickly as possible. We didn't want to move that far away from Boulder, but we were in a hurry to find a place, and we knew we didn't want to go into debt too badly from my writing sabbatical. That leads us to the day where Rachel's unpacking a boxful of plates and trying to tell herself this place really isn't that bad. She's trying to be assured that everything is going to be okay. I wrapped my arms around her, to be assuring, to ease all of her fears, because the truth was we were going to be okay.

I just had to prove that to my wife. I had to show her that she could put her faith in me and I'd lead us to the right place. We were all feeling better by the end of the night as Adam and I unloaded the last of the boxes from that U-Haul. When we finished the job, all four of us sat on the carpet in the living room and ate pizza as the sun set. We laughed, we told stories, and oddly enough, we felt at home even amidst the wood paneling. Life was moving fast for us now. Tomorrow morning the kids would start school, and once they were on the bus, I would come home and begin my novel. I took another bite of pizza and felt fulfilled. These next six months were going to fly by. It was like we were all sitting in the front car of a roller coaster. The coaster had been slowly clicking up the tracks, but now it was at its apex and ready to start plummeting down. Soon we would all be shouting screams of joy as our coaster soared into a pitch-black tunnel.

3

Progressive Evil

That next morning I walked into my office and took out the outline for my novel. The cover page of the outline read "Progressive Evil." I got the idea last spring when Rachel and I were invited to a progressive dinner in our old neighborhood. If you've never been to a progressive dinner, it's kind of like a potluck except the food stays at home and it's the people who move from place to place. In one home we had appetizers, in the next we had an Asian chopped salad, then we had steaks, and finally the party moved to our house where we all ate the chocolate soufflés Rachel made for dessert. It was a nice evening, and it was interesting to get to know the personalities of our neighbors as we went from one home to the next. But that's also what made the evening a little jarring. Every home was decorated so differently. Every mantel had photographs, and obviously the people were different in each home, but the photography was just as different. Some photos were modern and in black and white, with the families standing in front of old buildings, and others were the types where the family gets dressed up, goes to Sears, and snaps some photos in front of a paper backdrop.

But most of all, every home *felt* so different.

You've experienced this before, I'm sure. Just by walking into a house you're able to tell what the conversations at the dinner table are like; you can tell if the discussion centered around what was on the front page of that morning's *New York Times* or if sitcoms are blaring in the background while everyone chows down on dinner. And as you walk inside you know if the owners burn cinnamon candles, or if they clean with Pine-Sol, or if children have smashed Goldfish Crackers and Cheerios into the carpet. Sometimes if you're perceptive enough, you feel like the home has secrets to tell you. You begin to wonder what really happens when the doors are closed and the curtains are drawn.

This is where I got the idea for my story. I always tell my students that the question "What if?" is a great launching pad for any story. And so I thought, What if a family had to go to a progressive dinner and learn secrets about themselves in every home?

This was the inspiration. When I opened the outline, I read the following:

> James and Kelly have lived in the same home since they had children. They had the same friends, the same neighbors, and the same family. But one day James gets news that rocks their family to its core.
>
> He's being transferred.
>
> They've always lived near the mountains of Utah, but

now they're being forced to move across the country to a small town in Georgia. They end up in a small southern town and a neighborhood where everyone seems as close as a cult. The Davis family can't understand why they are so excluded. Finally one of the neighbors tells them, "Well, it's just because you haven't been to our progressive dinner yet. Once you come to that you'll understand who we really are."

Jim and Kelly Davis finally get the invite to the progressive dinner. They dress in their nicest outfits. Kelly makes her best dessert because the party is supposed to end at the Davis home.

Quickly they learn they've gotten more than they've bargained for. It starts out innocently enough. Cocktails and mingling and everyone getting to know one another. Then the host of the first home says, "We're going to play a game. It's called light as a feather, stiff as a board." Jim and Kelly look up at each other concerned. What is this game? "Kelly, we'd like you to go first." Kelly walks to the center. She has no idea what going first means. "Lie down," the host says.

Jim is uncomfortable as Kelly lies on the ground and the group circles around her, but he just waits to see what's going to happen. Kelly is told a frightening story by the host of the party and then all in the party begin to chant, "Light as a feather, stiff as a board," over and over. Jim sits helplessly on the couch as he watches the other couples lift Kelly off the floor. She is being held up, but just barely; everyone is lifting her using nothing more than two fingers. It looks like she is levitating.

This is too much.

Jim decides they need to leave. But before he can tell Kelly anything, it's his turn to play. He is told a story as well, but this one hits too close to home. This is a story about a family that moves to a small town and after two months of being there they go to a progressive dinner. Then the host of the dinner says, "And the couple's children have been kidnapped. The only way this couple will ever see their children again is to complete the progressive dinner."

Jim opens his eyes and stands up. He won't even let himself be levitated. He looks at the host who's telling this story and says, "Okay, I know we're the new couple and maybe this is some sort of hazing. But where we're from you don't joke about kidnapping someone's kids."

"Around here you don't joke about that either. That's why we're not joking. I know you were thinking about leaving, Jim. And we just can't have that. Not when we've gone to so much work to make this evening special for you."

"What are you talking about?" Kelly says.

"We have your children," the host smiles.

That smile gave me the shivers. I could picture the host looking at James and Kelly — staring right through their vulnerable innocent souls — and smiling. The couple wouldn't know what to do, but they'd have to keep going through the dinner. That was the beauty of the novel. Each house would get a little more horrific and James and Kelly would have to survive everything thrown at them for the sake of their children. It was the perfect setup, the type of story you'd see on the front shelves of Barnes and Noble. I could almost picture people coming into the bookstore and seeing *Progressive Evil* written in a scary red font. They'd grab the novel, open it up, and the jacket copy would be so gripping they'd have to read the book.

I was getting ahead of myself. I had to write the book first. So that day, after I dropped the children off and Rachel was still unpacking our pots and pans, I began to type. The words, sentences, and paragraphs came easily because I was using my own experiences to create. I could empathize with the insecurity of moving into a new neighborhood and not knowing anyone. Having all of this anxiety about moving my family into a strange place (even it was just forty minutes away) was fuel for creating the story. I didn't mean to make my family feel uncomfortable for the sake of my story; it was just a happy accident. It meant I didn't have to spend all of this work imagining what the characters would feel. I could just pluck the feelings from my own thought life, magnify them, and then put them through the lens of Jim and Kelly. This made my opening chapters come to life. I spent the first two weeks—

(Five months, two weeks left; better keep it up, Charlie.)

—crafting the opening chapters that I just described. When the week was over I had five chapters of original Charles Walker prose. I took everything I'd written and combed through it with my green pen and then fixed all the mistakes and inconsistencies. I spent the next week working on the chapters that describe what happens to our heroes in the first house.

That's where things went off track.

I was describing "light as a feather, stiff as a board,"* but I'd never played the game for myself. I thought it would be a cool way to first introduce the supernatural into my novel. The problem was I didn't know how to play the game, what the rules were, what it felt like, or what about it was particularly scary. I researched the game, but my knowledge was secondhand and distant and it showed in my writing. At first I thought maybe this was all just in my head. I was getting a little insecure now that I'd been writing for a couple of weeks and I just needed a little feedback.

I joined an online writing group and they confirmed what I was saying. They loved the setup, the opening chapters, and the introduction of the characters, but once I started talking about the first house, as one writer in the group put it, everything just got lame.

He said, *Honestly, once we get into the house things SHOULD start to get interesting, but this is when I was the most bored.*

He wasn't alone. This was the sentiment of nearly everyone in our group.

Another writer told me: *I've read scarier scenes in* Anne of Green Gables.

I wanted to be a horror writer and I was being compared

---

*"Light as a feather, stiff as a board" is a game played at parties. Some say it's tied to the occult. The game works like this: one person lies on the floor and is told a story of a woman who died in a car wreck on an icy road (or for the purposes of my novel, I had the group make up their own stories). After the story a group member says something to the effect of, "When they found the woman she was light as a feather, stiff as a board." They then repeat this phrase around twenty times, until the group members can lift ("levitate") the person in the air using only two fingers. The person is literally scared stiff in order to levitate.

to *Anne of Green Gables.* What was next? Would a writer in my group tell me chapter 7 reminded him of *Sarah, Plain and Tall?* Would they say my finale was a screamfest like *The Notebook?*

I needed a second opinion.

I printed off my work-in-progress and walked downstairs to give it to Rachel. She was watching TV when I walked into the living room. She barely watched TV at night in our old home. Seemed like after the kids went to bed she was always planning some get-together for the weekend or scrapbooking or talking on the phone with a friend in her mommy play-group. Now, she just sat on the couch and watched whatever weeknight prime-time television had to offer. I was glad I came down with my novel to rescue her. When I handed it over she said, "Is this ..."

"It's *Progressive Evil*," I said.

"Wow." Rachel's *wow* wasn't sarcastic; rather it was the wow of a wife who was really touched that I was finally letting her read what I had been so protective of in the last few weeks. "Can I read it?"

"Of course you can read it," I said.

"I'm going to love it," she said.

"You can't say that."

"Why not?"

"Because then you have to love it. And I don't want you to have to do anything," I said.

"So what should I say?"

"Don't say anything. Just read it."

I sat there and at first I was unbelievably anxious as she

read. I was trying to read *Cujo*, but I couldn't pay attention to the novel. I needed to see the looks on Rachel's face. I was trying to see when was she swept up by the story. When was she afraid? When was she on the edge of her seat wondering exactly what would happen next? I needed to stop. I turned my attention toward the wood paneling on the wall. I had expected it to grow on me; maybe I'd even start to appreciate it for its unique qualities. It did not grow on me. It was more like the annoying guy who talked really loudly on the phone one cubicle over or the roommate who never did the dishes.

Finally Rachel looked up. She'd finished reading. "What'd you think?" I asked.

"It was good."

"Good."

"Yeah, really good."

"Anything else?" I asked.

"I loved the first few chapters."

"And then what?"

"I don't know. It's hard to say."

"You hated it."

"No, I didn't hate it. The writing was warm, and the descriptions were beautiful; it's just, I don't know ..."

"Tell me," I said.

"I just thought it was supposed to be scary."

"I didn't think you liked scary stories," I said.

"I don't. Not really. That's why I kept bracing myself to be really scared. And then it didn't happen."

"You were never scared?"

"No, not really. I mean, the setup was so good. When

they'd been told their kids were kidnapped, I thought it was about to get scary."

"And what about the rest of it?"

"I thought it was interesting."

"But not scary?" I asked.

"No. Not even a little. And that was kind of a letdown."

"What would make it scarier?"

"I don't know. Maybe if you added vampires."

"I can't add vampires."

"Why not? It's your book. You can add anything you want."

"I know, but vampires aren't the point of the story," I said.

"I thought the point of the story was to be scary."

"Well, it is."

"And vampires are scary," she said.

"Okay. Yeah, I'll think about adding vampires," I said.

"Zombies are also pretty scary."

"Okay, thank you, honey," I said. "That's really interesting feedback." But what my tone implied was, *You're annoying. Please stop destroying my novel.* I didn't mean to be so snippy. It's just, I'm a writer and we have such fragile egos when it comes to our own stories. We give people our stories and we ask for feedback, and some part of us wants constructive criticism, but in the moment all we really want is for people to throw roses and tell us how brilliant we are. That's what I wanted my wife to do. I wanted her to cheer me on, not try to turn my story into *The Addams Family.*

Rachel could tell how badly she'd hurt me. She said, "I'm sure you've really polished the first chapters and these just need to be polished a little more."

"Yeah, that's true," I said, even though it wasn't true at all. If anything, I'd worked on the later chapters twice as much as anything else. And those were the chapters she said needed more vampires and zombies. And this is my wife who thinks *Grey's Anatomy* is too scary to watch. I couldn't talk about this anymore. I said, "I mean everything is a first draft."

"Exactly," she added. "Charlie, all of it is good. Really."

"Thank you," I said. I took the pages from her and quickly thumbed through them as if I was looking for the part that wasn't scary. As if I could write a quick note: "Be scarier here" and fix it in the morning.

She looked at me flipping through the manuscript and said, "It's just, if those other chapters could be a little more frightening. I was never frightened. I always felt safe. I don't know. I wish I could explain it a little better," she said.

"No, that's good. I got it," I said. I didn't get it, but I wanted my wife to stop talking. I left our wood-paneled living room and carried the manuscript up to my office, not really sure what to do with it.

4

Reflection

I woke up, put on my robe, brewed my coffee, cracked open my laptop, and placed my fingers on the keyboard ready to write. Today I would fix all of the problems that Rachel highlighted last night. Once those were solved, I'd blaze ahead and create terrifying new moments and situations for the Davis family to face. That was the plan anyway. I just couldn't find the inspiration. I reread all that I'd written and then stared at the computer screen. My cup of coffee was slurped empty before I'd even written one new word. My story was in trouble, and I knew it, even if I didn't want to admit it.

I went downstairs and poured another cup of coffee. I didn't want to go back up to the office. I opened the sliding glass door in our kitchen and walked into the backyard. I looked around at our flimsy wooden fence and this giant elm tree that's roots were bulging from the ground, killing all of the grass (and by grass, I mean mostly weeds) around it.

And in the corner of the backyard there was this white metal shed coated in rust. *I needed to get a lock to put on that thing and tell the kids never to go in it. They'd probably get spider bites and tetanus if they ever stepped in there.*

The morning air was cold, and I stood there in my T-shirt, my robe, and my pinstriped boxers, unsure of what to do with myself. What was wrong with me? I was a horror writer who couldn't write a scary story. Rachel wanted me to add vampires and zombies to the story. This wasn't supposed to be that kind of story. This wasn't a horror novel for preteen girls. This was supposed to be a sophisticated psychological thriller. Sophisticated psychological thrillers don't have vampires and zombies.*

I took a deep breath. Steam wafted from my coffee cup as I surveyed my surroundings. My thoughts went away from my novel and on to how hopeless things were for us. Why did I move to this house? I should have never quit my job. This whole thing was going to end badly. We were going to have a bunch of debt, and what if the school wouldn't hire me back? What if any school wouldn't hire—

"Good morning," a voice said. It came from a man in the neighboring yard who'd just walked out onto his deck. I was assuming he was my neighbor. I couldn't say for sure because I hadn't been very social since we'd moved in, and now there was some guy in his backyard saying hi to me and wearing

---

*I stand corrected. With further research, I've found there are quite a few sophisticated thrillers with zombies. But you'd be hard-pressed to find a sophisticated thriller with vampires.

very cool jeans.* In fact, his jeans were so cool that I would have been embarrassed by my own jeans if I were wearing any. Luckily, I wasn't wearing any pants at all, just my flannel bathrobe and white T-shirt.

"Good morning," I replied, lifting my coffee cup in the air.

"Welcome to the neighborhood," the man in jeans said.

"We're just renting," I said. I didn't want to imply that I didn't like the neighborhood, just that we had better taste in homes and we'd never buy a home like the one we were in unless we were going to remodel it. And we weren't going to remodel, because like I said, we were just renting.

"If you guys need anything, let me know. I'm Blake."

"Charlie," I replied.

"Good to meet you, Charlie."

"You too, Blake."

"Have you guys had any problems with the house?" Blake asked.

"Like what problems?"

"Nothing really. It's just the last two people who've lived there didn't last very long. They move in quickly and then they move out quickly." Blake paused.

"Oh. Um, I didn't know that," I said.

"Right, well it's probably just the economy. Seems like half

---

*You learn quite a bit about jeans when you teach high school. You learn they are not a fashion accessory — they are *the* fashion accessory. Learning how to spot a wash, style, and cut of jeans becomes second nature after a while. I'm sure it's the same way that someone who was raised in an Amish community can spot well-churned butter from poorly churned butter.

our country is moving around like gypsies these days looking for work. That's why I'm grateful for my steady job."

"What do you do?" I asked.

"I work with the Castle Rock Fire Department. You?"

"I'm a writer," I said. It felt weird to have my new occupation cross my lips. Just admitting this out loud made our new life seem somehow more official.

"What sort of things do you write? Like magazines or books—"

"Books," I said. I really hoped at that moment he wouldn't ask if I'd had any published. I really hoped at that moment I wouldn't have to explain my situation to a complete stranger.

"What kind of books?" Blake asked.

"Novels."

"Is that fiction or nonfiction?"

"Fiction," I said. "I write horror novels."

"Wow, that sounds scary."

"Hopefully it will be," I said.

"Well, welcome to the neighborhood," Blake said. "Would you guys like to come over for dinner later this week? My wife's making lasagna on Thursday. She makes great lasagna, but we always have a lot left over. There'd be more than enough to feed both of our families."

I was a little taken aback that he'd invited us for dinner so quickly. In my experience, people dressed like Blake don't go out of their way to make friends. But his offer was so generous I thought maybe this is exactly what we needed. If we made friends with our neighbors, then our house would feel a little more, well, like home. "Yeah, we'd love to. Thank you," I told Blake. "What can we bring?"

"How about dessert or something?"

"Sounds good," I said.

* * *

"What kind of dessert? Did he say what kind, or what their family likes, or what they normally eat for dessert with lasagna?" Rachel asked.

"He just said dessert."

"Okay, well I'll just have to find something then. What kind of dessert goes well with lasagna?"

"Chocolate cake," I said.

"Chocolate cake is the most unimaginative dessert we could bring. I mean, why even make chocolate cake? Let's just bring a bucket of generic vanilla ice cream while we're at it. Or let's just bring a bag of Oreos."

"No, we shouldn't bring Oreos," I said even though it sounded convenient to bring Oreos and I'm sure the kids would have loved them.

"I'll just find something to bake." Rachel then spent the next three hours online looking at dessert possibilities: S'mores cupcakes, cream cheese key lime pie, white chocolate soufflé with a raspberry glaze, the list went on and on. After her hours of searching she then spent another two hours in the grocery store and two more hours getting all of her ingredients organized so she could make a decadent tiramisu for dinner the next day.

Rachel's day was twelve times more productive than mine. I spent the afternoon looking at my computer trying to write, but my fears—

(You can't write anything good because you don't have anything

45

good in you. Who do you think you are? You're just some English teacher. What, you actually think you can quit your job and then magically just sit down and write a bestseller? No one's going to read your book, Charlie. You're going to spend six months—or years even—on this thing and then no one other than a few of your friends is going to read it. And even your friends won't read it, they'll just smile and say they did out of pity.)

—about the novel were growing. I spent a few more hours trying to write, but finally Rachel came into the room and said, "Come on, let's go to bed."

But I couldn't even sleep right. I sat in bed with my eyes wide open. I was trying to forget about the book, the day; I was trying to just get some sleep so I could start over tomorrow. I couldn't. Too many thoughts were racing through my head, including something my neighbor told me that morning: *The last two people who've lived there didn't last very long. They move in quickly and then they move out quickly.* What did he mean by that? Was there really something wrong with this house? What if something horrible had already happened in here? What if I moved my wife into a place where someone came in on Christmas morning and started spraying shotgun blasts everywhere? Maybe that's why I got this house so cheaply.

I've always been a calm academic sort of guy; like I said, I was the guy never picked for the baseball team. I never got into fights or confrontations because I knew I would lose. I knew the only way to win was to avoid conflict altogether. But what if some freak walked up the stairs to where my family was sleeping—

46

And that's when I heard a door click shut. I rolled over and looked at the clock.

12:45.

I lay in bed for a moment, realizing I didn't have a gun and I hadn't installed an alarm system. I thought nothing was going to happen to us. Bad things were what happened to other people. But something wasn't in other people's homes right now. Something was in my home. It was forty-five minutes after midnight and there was a click. Where did it come from? Rachel was next to me and she'd been asleep for at least an hour. Maybe Adam and Lucy had gotten up to get a drink or something.

I rolled out of bed and slid my feet into my slippers. I put on my bathrobe and tied it shut. If there was someone in my house, for some reason I was concerned that he was going to see me in my pajamas. *Never mind that, he's here to rob and/or kill you, Charlie.* Just breathe, I thought. Check on your kids. Everything's fine.

I peeked in Adam's room, and he was out. He hadn't moved since I'd put him to bed. Same with Lucy. She was surrounded by an army of stuffed animals. She couldn't have gotten up or she would have knocked them over. I was just imagining things. It was probably —

Creak.

It was the floor downstairs. And we were all up here. Which meant someone was down there. I stood upstairs and thought about my worst fear coming true. Someone was in my house. He wanted to hurt every member of my family. Adam, Lucy, Rachel — he would go after all of them. At moments like these I always wished I owned a gun — even though every other moment of my life I was completely against owning a firearm. I've always heard something like, "You're much more likely to have one of your family injured with a gun than you are to injure someone in your home." That's a nice thought 99 percent of the time until a crazy axe murderer is in your home and you don't have anything to protect yourself with.

That was me.

No way to protect myself or my family. Just standing upstairs waiting for someone to appear. Rachel would scream and then it would be too late. I would cry and tell the cops, "I should have bought a gun. Why didn't I buy a gun?"

It was ridiculous. I was playing out the whole scenario before anything ever even happened. This was the problem with being a writer, especially a horror writer. You create the worst possible story all the time. I knew I needed to stop. I knew I just needed to go downstairs and find out what—

(Don't you mean who?)

—was making that sound. I put on my robe and walked downstairs. I didn't like my home this late at night. It felt claustrophobic, as if furniture and picture frames were reaching at me. It felt like there was so much clutter that I could miss whatever was really hiding in the shadows.

I walked into the living room. It was dark. Silent.

The TV flicked on.

There was an infomercial. "You're going to love what we turn you into," the guy in the toupee exclaimed. The audience clapped for his statement like a bunch of drugged-up lemmings. "You may not be happy with who you are, but wait until you see what you become!" the host shouted at me.

I turned from the TV and scanned the living room. Lucy's baby doll, Ainslie, sat in the recliner and the glow of the TV flickered off its face. The doll was grinning at me.

The TV flicked to blue.

It was a solid blue screen. There was no static and snow like in *Poltergeist*. In the screen I saw my reflection. I was frozen when my reflection started to move. There was someone in here right behind me. I couldn't make out exactly what the person in the reflection looked like, but I could smell his breath. When I looked at the reflection more carefully, I could see a knife in his hand, and I could see he was smiling; he wanted me to know he was completely demented and without reservation for what he was about to do. I couldn't move. This freak broke into my home to take everything from my family and I couldn't move.

(Turn around. You can't just stand there. Do something. He's going to kill you if you don't turn around.)

I forced myself to spin around—

He wasn't there. There was no one holding the remote or a knife. I turned back to the TV. It was just a bright blue screen. I glanced next to the couch and the remote was on the floor. I turned on every lamp in the living room. Nothing. I checked to make sure the front and the back doors were locked. They were. The windows were all closed. I kept searching, but there was no one in my house.

It was just too wild an imagination—

(Can your imagination change the TV channel?)

—and too much stress. I was still shaking. There is nothing more invasive than someone breaking into your home. The thought of some freak breaking in here and rummaging through our things was so violating. Just the thought of his hands on my TV remote, my silverware, the thought of him in here seeing pictures of my family at Disneyland made me shiver.

And then it inspired me.

I suddenly knew how to fix the chapters Rachel hated in *Progressive Evil.* Kelly and James need to walk into the next home and see the living room decorated with their coffee table, their TV, their half-burnt yellow candle with a vanilla cupcake smell. Maybe that room would even be decorated with pictures from their wedding and family vacation to Lake Tahoe. That would be creepy. These people weren't just controlling James and Kelly's kids; they were controlling everything.

I didn't want to go back to sleep. I shut the door to the office and started to write. The story poured out of me as if it wasn't even from me, as if I were pulling this story out of some sacred place that only the worthiest of authors like Updike and King and Faulkner are allowed to enter. I wrote through the night.

The sun rose.

I didn't even know what time it was when Rachel flicked on the light in the study and asked, "Wow, honey, you got up early. What are you doing?"

The Black Cauldron

Now, before you go off and start thinking—well, whatever it is you're thinking about me right now—you need to understand I wasn't trying to live out my novel. I didn't want my kids to actually be kidnapped so I would know what it was like to have my kids kidnapped. I didn't want Rachel and me to be in harm's way so I would know what it would feel like to be in real danger. I just needed to get a sniff of what the feeling was.

My writing wasn't scary because I wasn't scared.

Thinking there was that invader in my house gave me fear to feed off of. It made my writing come alive. And when I first got into writing I used real emotions to create. In fact, processing my emotions is the reason I got into writing anyway. It was in high school and I'd been morose, depressed, and withdrawn ever since Mom had died. Dad sent me to counseling, but talking about my feelings didn't help. Talking about it only made the fears worse. But when I was a junior in high school we were reading *Young Goodman Brown*, a story about a man who goes into the forest late one night, runs into the devil, and discovers that his wife was secretly a witch. My English teacher gave us an option—we could either write a three-page report on the story or a five-page short story of our own. Most students chose the report because it required fewer pages. I chose the story—it ended up being fifteen pages long. My English teacher, Mr. Peretti, asked me to stay after class two days later.

"Charlie, did you really write this?"

"Yeah," I said.

"There's a literary journal that a colleague of mine is putting together at another high school. He wants to collect all of the best poetry and short stories from students all around Denver. Would you mind if I sent him this?"

"No. That'd be cool," I said. I always hated using slang around Mr. Peretti, but what was I supposed to say? That would be "splendid" or "stupendous"? I was just a junior and it *was cool.*

My story got published in that school journal and the writing saved me. I kept writing in college; that's one of the things Rachel loved about me when we first met. And when I was courting Rachel, it was the angst of young love and the warmth of her attention that fueled my prose. But in my comfortable day-to-day life I'd gotten away from any sort of pain or fear. I needed that sort of high emotion to create worthwhile stories. I needed to understand things.

The chapters everyone hated fell flat because I didn't understand the supernatural. I was writing about a cult that played evil games and used Ouija boards, but I'd never played those games and I'd never been to a séance.

Which is how I found myself in a store called the Black Cauldron. It was this shop in downtown Denver I must have walked by a hundred times before but never noticed. The place was filled with books of spells, decorative skull heads, Ouija boards, and all sorts of other things I'd never been exposed to. I picked up the cheapest Ouija board I could find. It wasn't like I was expecting to use it a lot. I'd just use it once—

(This is just what you need.)

—so I could construct my next chapter. I had this scene in mind where the hosts at the next house of the party start using a Ouija board and inanimate objects begin to float all around the room. I tried to write the scene without inspiration, and the chapter felt as limp and scripted as reality television. I could picture giving Rachel these chapters and her shrugging and saying, "This is good, Charlie." But I'd know what she really meant: *This isn't any good. We've sacrificed our future for this?*

I wasn't going to let that happen. I wasn't going to let our sacrifice be for nothing. I picked up the Ouija board and walked to the front of the store. The guy behind the counter didn't look particularly gothic or demonic. With his beige sweater and perfectly coiffed hair, he looked more likely to create a chai latte than to summon the prince of darkness. Still, I felt intimidated and guilty walking up there with this Ouija board in my hand. This guy was clearly going to be able to tell I was a rookie who had no idea what he was doing.

I laid my Ouija board on the counter and the clerk asked me, "Is that all for you?"

"Yes," I answered, but then I wondered what sort of accessories people are supposed to buy with Ouija boards. *Actually, I'll take a pack of tarot cards and that ornate knife for sacrificing goats too.*

"Are you sure this is the board you want?" the clerk asked.

"Why wouldn't it be?"

"Well, what are you using it for?" the clerk asked.

Is there more than one use for a Ouija board? Can you also play monopoly on them? *All I really want to do is scare myself a little, understand what it feels like to use a board so I can turn right around and write about it.* But I didn't say that out loud. He might lecture me about using Ouija boards for research, and I really didn't feel like getting a browbeating from some barista who works for Satan.

"I'm using it for a séance," I said.

"What all are you planning on doing at the séance?" he said.

"What are my options?"

"Well, there are some boards that are better conduits for talking with friends and family. And there are other boards that are better for talking with distant dead."

"The distant dead?"

"You know—kings, presidents, Joan of Arc—people like that."

"Really?"

"Really," the clerk said.

"So what's this board good for?" I asked.

"It's good for scaring junior high kids at slumber parties."

"Okay," I said. Just what I needed—a sarcastic clerk at the occult store. Still, he made me think twice. I considered walking back there and buying the most expensive of boards so I could talk to Mark Twain or Queen Elizabeth if I ever needed to. Then I realized how stupid that was. *What are you doing?* I thought. I didn't believe any of this stuff. You can't talk to the dead because dead people are dead. A thousand-dollar Ouija board won't make them any less dead than one that costs $9.99. Either way, you'll just be sitting there with candles flickering, talking into a darkness that can't answer. Satan's barista was just trying to con me out of more money.

"You know what, this one will be just fine," I said. Then I didn't say another thing as I paid for my board and left the Black Cauldron.

As I turned a corner, I ran into some guy in a business suit. He was tall, had curly blond hair, and a commanding presence to him. "Excuse me," he said.

"Sorry," I replied. I wasn't sure whose fault it was, but I'll apologize for nearly anything, even if it isn't my fault.

"Don't worry about it. Hey, do you have the time?" he said.

I took out my cell phone. "It's 1:30," I said. I couldn't believe in this day and age anybody still needed to ask for the time. From the way this guy was dressed you'd think he'd have a Rolex and a couple of iPhones on him.

"Thanks," he said and then peered into my bag. The Ouija board was hanging out in plain sight. "Been doing a little shopping?"

"Yeah. I just bought this. It's not for me. I mean, I don't talk to dead people or anything." I couldn't believe I was here trying to justify my purchase to this large blond man.

"No, I'm sure there are lots of other uses for those things," he said.

"Well, I'm using it for research."

"What line of work are you in?"

"I'm a writer. Books. I write novels."

"Let me guess, horror?"

"Yes, exactly," I said.

"Where do you do your writing? Do you have an office?"

"No, I write from home."

"Oh, you do? So you're taking that home?"

"Um, yeah ..."

"Do you have kids?"

"Two. A boy and a girl." I paused. "Oh, I see what you're getting at. No, they'll never know I have this. It's just for research."

"Right. You said that already. Well, I'm sure you'll be fine. Listen, it was really nice meeting you, but I have to run."

"See you later," I said and watched the annoying blond man run off.

When I got home, for the second time in a half hour I felt guilty about my new purchase. I was unloading the board out of my car when I looked over at Blake's. He was shutting the garage behind him. He looked up at me and shouted, "Charlie," as the door came to the ground. "Are we still good for dinner tonight?"

"Yeah, we're planning on it. Rachel's been working all day on dessert," I said.

Blake took his eyes off me and glanced at the Ouija board in my hands. His body stiffened and he was clearly uncomfortable. But he didn't want me to know he was uncomfortable. He either thought it'd be rude to judge me for holding a Ouija board or he was scared I'd cast a spell on him. I wasn't sure because all he told me was, "Just bring yourself and your beautiful family. We should have enough food for everyone."

"Okay," I said.

"Okay then," Blake echoed.

* * *

At 5:30 we knocked on Blake's front door. Rachel was holding the tiramisu and we were all dressed up nicely. I guess you could say we were in business casual attire. My kids had exactly two outfits that would classify as business casual because, well, they were kids. But Blake seemed like a classy guy, so I thought it would be good for us to err on the side of overdressed.

"Come in. I'm Tammy," said the woman who answered the door. Tammy was as hip as her husband; she had a fashionable top and her hair was highlighted in all of the right places. I scanned the house and saw most of the things you'd expect from a couple like this—a well-kept house, swanky lampshades, and leather furniture. But as we made our way into the house, I saw something that, well, I had never seen anything quite like it. It was a framed painting of a building on fire and a group of firemen were holding the hose spraying out the fire. I don't normally see paintings of firemen, but if that was all, it would have just been mildly bizarre. What really made this painting stand out, however, was that alongside all of the firemen, Jesus was there also holding the hose and helping out. He wasn't wearing a bright yellow hat or anything—he was dressed in traditional Jesus clothes and he seemed to be whispering something to one of the firemen. Tammy must have noticed me staring at the painting because she said, "Yeah, Blake's a firefighter."

As if the firefighters were the noteworthy part of the portrait. I was taken aback by this painting. Who exactly were these people? Was I in for a weird evening? I thought surely someone could have a portrait like this, I just didn't think people in designer jeans loved Jesus that much. I looked for other Jesus items in their home. On their shelf were the Bible and *Left Behind* (I was pretty sure the plot of that book involved Jesus riding a horse through on a white cloud to reign over the earth), but there were also classic works of literature like Twain and Dickens. The painting and the books were the only Jesus things I noticed, otherwise their home was as stylish as their jeans, as if Blake and Tammy had a running tab at Pottery Barn and Crate and Barrel.

The night didn't go strangely. Actually, it couldn't have gone better. The four adults sat at a table eating this great lasagna and salad while our kids ate with Blake's kids. After dinner the kids played video games in their den while we talked about health care, TV shows, and parenting. We ate Rachel's tiramisu and everyone adored it. Rachel acted like it was no big deal, but clearly she loved the praise from such fashionable and nice people.

As the evening was winding down, it felt like we were old friends. Or at the very least it felt like we were forming a new friendship — which is why Rachel got so upset with me when I asked our hosts, "Okay, really, I've got to know, why is Jesus putting out the fire?"

"Jesus isn't putting out the fire," Blake said.

"Well, what's he doing? Cheering them on?" I asked. Rachel squeezed my leg under the table, which was code for, *Charlie, stop whatever it is you're doing right now.*

"Have you ever put out a fire, Charlie?" Blake's voice was firm but compassionate. It felt like I'd just slid over a soapbox for him to stand on.

"I started a few when I was eight. Can't say I've ever put one out."

"It's pretty intimidating," Blake said. "A whole building or house on fire, and you don't know if it's going to collapse, if there are people in there, if you're going to have to risk never seeing your family again by running to someone's rescue. When I first became a firefighter, the fear was paralyzing. I joined when I was young because I thought it'd be an exciting career. But when I faced the real pressures of the job, I didn't know if I could handle it. But the thought of Jesus being there with me to provide me strength and courage helped me through things. This painting was done by a friend at our church, and it's just a metaphor and a reminder of that."

"Um ... wow, that's great," I said. I felt like a jerk. I might as well have been making fun of his dead grandmother. And I wasn't trying to make fun of the thing; it's just not every day that you see pictures of Jesus reenacting one of the scenes from *Backdraft.*

"Can I ask you a question now?"

"Sure," I said.

"What are you going to do with that Ouija board?" Blake asked.

"He doesn't have a Ouija board," Rachel said.

"Well, I just bought one," I corrected.

"You bought what?"

"It's not that big of a deal. I got the cheapest one they had," I said. I thought the bargain price of the board would show everyone my lack of commitment and care for all things of the occult.

"Why?" Rachel asked.

"For research. I'm using it to help me write one of the scenes for *Progressive Evil*." Everyone was staring at me. It's one thing to question Jesus and the firemen, but now I owned a Ouija board. What sort of spawn of Satan was I? "I don't even believe in the things," I added.

"I believe in them," Blake replied.

"You do? Do you have one? Could you show me how to use it because I really have no idea?"

"No, I believe in them, which is why I don't have one. You don't want to mess with that stuff, Charlie. It's real."

"Come on, it's just a game people use to make their parties a little more interesting. Do you really think if I use the thing to call on Jimi Hendrix he'll show up to play the national anthem with his teeth?" I wish I did believe that could happen because it sounded kind of cool.

"I don't know what will come into the room. I just wouldn't want to bring any of that stuff near my family."

(Well, I don't have anyone over my shoulders whispering me ideas and scenes for my novel. That's not a luxury us ordinary people have. I have to write the thing entirely by myself. I've quit my job and put my family in jeopardy. That's the risk that we're facing.

That's what my reality is.)

This was what sprung into my head. But Rachel was already upset with me because of everything I'd said, and besides, these were good people who'd let us into their home. I was just feeling a little defensive. So I said, "I only bought the thing on a whim anyway. I don't know if I was really even planning to use it."

6

Séance for One

I wasn't sure if Rachel was asleep.

At least I wasn't sure if she was in a deep sleep, the type of sleep where I could leave the room and she would have no idea that I'd ever been gone. Does she even sleep that deeply? You'd think after thirteen years of marriage I would know, but I'd never sneaked around on my wife before. Okay, that's not entirely true. But I'd only committed misdemeanors in our marriage. Never a felony. I had a Sherlock Holmes pipe that I used to sneak out to the garage and smoke in the early days of my writing. She didn't understand why I would do something that would make my clothes stink that badly, and I didn't understand how mimicking anything Sherlock Holmes did could be frowned upon. I'd sneak to the garage, then wash my hands, brush my teeth, and pretend that nothing had happened. Inevitably she'd kiss me and say, "You've been smoking that pipe, haven't you?"

"How could you smell that? I brushed my teeth and chewed gum."

"I could smell it in your nostrils."

Checkmate. Elementary, my dear Charlie.

This is how things went with Rachel. She could always sense when I was up to no good. I'm not sure how, but I knew she'd be able to smell the stench of the Ouija board if I went downstairs and used it. Which, honestly, was kind of annoying. I didn't even think it was that big of a deal or that anyone would care when I bought the thing.

But after we got home from Blake's and put our kids to bed, we were in the middle of our bedtime ritual. I was doing push-ups on the floor and she was brushing her teeth. Mid brush, with her mouth full of toothpaste, she looked at me and said, "You need to take that thing back."

"The Ouija board?"

"Yes," she said.

"Do you believe in that stuff?"

"What stuff?"

"I don't know, Ouija board stuff," I said.

"It's just not a good thing to have around. Adam and Lucy could get the wrong idea and then start wanting to use it, and then they'll start hanging out with kids dressed in black who wear eye makeup."

"I won't do it around our kids," I said.

"Why is this that big of a deal?"

"It's not. I'm just using it as research. I'm a little stumped on this chapter."

"Why can't you just read some articles online for research?" Rachel asked.

"Reading articles isn't the same."

"Aren't you just trying to understand how a Ouija board works?"

"Yeah, but well, it's complicated, honey. I think I'm a method writer," I said.

"A method writer?"

"You know how some actors lose themselves completely in the part? Okay, I heard Health Ledger walked around for months as the Joker. I read Anthony Hopkins came to the set as Hannibal Lector. Everyone would call him Mr. Lector; he ate cheese Danishes on set as if he were a cannibal."

"I don't think that's true—"

"All I'm saying is they only had to create one character. I have to create an entire frightening world. So, I think if I can *experience* things, I can really write about them in a meaningful way."

"So is there a murder in your story? Is there an affair? Is there a terrorist bombing?"

I couldn't believe Rachel was resisting this so strongly. It didn't seem that creepy when I was using real life experiences before. Didn't Mark Twain say write what you know? But now Rachel was treating me like I was a member of the Donner party and/or Al Qaeda. She just didn't understand. She wasn't a writer. "No, you're right. I'll find some articles tomorrow and take the board back in the morning."

"Thank you," she said. And then we lay quietly in bed.

That's where I was with my head on my pillow waiting for her to fall asleep. When I couldn't lie there any longer I started to inch out of bed slowly until my feet hit the carpet. I slid on my slippers and put on my robe. Rachel stirred and

I froze. If she asked me where I was going I'd have to say something like, "to the bathroom," and then come back to bed. Then tomorrow I'd have to take the Ouija board back.

Luckily, my wife settled back onto her pillow. I waited another minute and finally crept out of our room and into the office. I grabbed some papers I'd printed earlier, then went to the kitchen to grab one of our candles. The board was sitting on our dining room table in this black plastic bag. I held the board and it seemed harmless. How could anything with the Parker Brothers logo on the side of the box be dangerous? This thing wasn't even as harmful as an Easy-Bake Oven. Kids could at least melt Ken and Barbie with one of those.

This is ridiculous. You should go back to bed.

And again, I probably should have, but I knew it was already too late. I was too curious. I had to find out what the Ouija board would do and if there was anything that could inspire my writing. Maybe this is why the people in horror movies make such bad decisions. They know it's a bad decision to go back into the house, or run up the stairs, or to assume that the serial killer is not a killer at all; it's just someone pulling a practical joke. People in horror movies know these are bad decisions, but the evil is pulling them in and they are powerless against it.

Wow, that's really good. You should write that down, I thought. Already this experience was helping me gain insight.

I went down to the basement. It was unfinished. Boxes were all over the place and it smelled like pink insulating fiber. I unwrapped the Ouija board and placed it onto the basement floor. The Parker Brothers board was cheap looking. It seemed to be about the same quality as Candy Land, only with less happy-looking candy people. How was this mass-produced piece of flimsy plastic going to help me write a bestselling novel? Maybe that clerk was right. I should have bought a real Ouija board. Something nice and carved out of wood. But then I wondered if Satan was real, would he care what the board was made out of? Are demonic forces really Ouija board snobs?

Once I was in the basement I lit the candle. I didn't turn on the lights for the sake of atmosphere. I sat down and grabbed the instructions that I'd printed out. There were instructions that came with the board, but they only told the "what" of how things worked and not the "why." I needed to really understand how this thing worked (or was supposed to work) to write about it. So I held my printed instructions closely and read them:

When beginning your Ouija board session, use only one white candle. Black candles symbolize evil. But a single white candle symbolizes goodness and hope and it will help you to have a more pleasurable séance.

My candle was yellow, from the Yankee Candle Company, and it had a "vanilla cupcake" aroma. I hoped that wouldn't be a problem. I wasn't sure what the preferred aroma for a séance was, but I doubted "vanilla cupcake" was at the top of the list.

Also, make sure to use your Ouija board at night. There is less interference at night.

Less interference. Whatever. I was ready to play along.

Very lightly place your fingers on the planchette. Then move it around some to get it warmed up.

Sure, I thought. The planchette was shaped like a little wooden heart with a glass circle in the center of it. Wherever I stopped it, it would highlight one letter in the alphabet or the words "yes" and "no." I moved it around, and it felt very much like I was the one moving it around. No spirits were guiding me. No evil forces taking control of my hands.

The medium should now begin by announcing that the session will only allow an experience that is positive or toward a higher good and that negative energies are not welcome.

Um, okay. Sure.

I looked at all the boxes in my basement and then listened once again to make sure Rachel or any of the kids hadn't woken up for any reason. Then I spoke, "This session is beginning now and so I only want this experience to be positive and toward the greater good. So, yeah, I'm the new guy here so don't do anything too creepy."

Decide on a person the group wants to speak to. Perhaps a family member or a friend.

I wasn't sure whom to speak with. I could ask to speak with my grandmother, but bringing her into my basement for a séance seemed utterly evil and awkward. Maybe I could try to speak with my mom. I stared at that vanilla cupcake candle and remembered praying for Mom. I remembered the last time I went to church the night she died. Now for the first time in thirty years I could call out to her. But what should I say? Maybe if this really worked and she was actually out there I could tell her a little bit about us. I could tell her that Adam looks just like her when he gets upset and that Lucy has her same photographic memory. I could tell her that they ask about their grandma and I talk to them about her all the time. I felt like I wanted to cry at this possibility, which made me upset with myself. What was I doing? Why was I torturing myself like this? I couldn't talk to my mother because she wasn't here. She was dead. And dead is dead, and there are no board games that bring dead people back to life.

But other than her, I wasn't sure whom to ask to speak with. Elvis? John Lennon? I just didn't know a lot of dead people. Or at least not a lot were coming to mind. I closed my eyes, thought through my life, and pictured caskets, flowers, ministers — anything to conjure up the thought of death.

That's when I saw something: Lana Morris, a girl I knew in high school. Actually *know* is much too strong of a word. I didn't know her. Nobody did. But I saw her every day for years. She'd sit in the corner and stare out the window or carve things into her desk. She had black hair and wore plain dingy clothes. Sometimes after class I'd linger around long enough for her to leave so I could see what she'd carved. It was always a single word: *hope, love, pain, fear, need.* Every word fraught with mystery and meaning. I always wanted to ask her about them. "What do you mean, *hope?* Why'd you carve *hope* into your desk? Why *love?* Why *fear?* Why *need?*"

But then I was in history one day and Lana wasn't there; no staring out the window, no new word freshly carved into her desk. By third period the rumors were swirling. Later that day there was an assembly where the principal announced that Lana had taken her life. Rumor was, a bottle of something, aspirin maybe, but nobody knew for sure.

Sitting on that basement floor, I remembered the funeral. I could see her lying in that casket with makeup caked onto her pale dead face. Not many kids from the school went, but I felt like I should be there. And with her in my thoughts, I said, "I want to speak to Lana Morris."

Begin simply. Start with a yes or no question.

"Lana, are you here?"

I half expected the feeling of evil to overtake the room. I lit the candle, started my session, and invited a dead high school classmate to come into my house. Isn't this when the darkness should rush in? Maybe. Maybe that's how it happened for other people.

But for me it didn't happen quite like that. I was being dipped into the evil. For instance, the thought of Lana coming into my mind—where did that come from? I hadn't thought of her for years. *Something* made me think of her. Whatever that something, it was subtle. It made me wonder if maybe evil forces understand that they can't reveal themselves to us all at once. Our fragile minds couldn't handle it. Maybe this is why all of us believe that we've seen and experienced evil—

(Throw the board away. Go to bed. Rachel's going to know what you're doing if you don't leave right now. You'll wake her up and she'll know what you did. And that's when she'll really start to worry.)

—yet we're not absolutely sure how exactly to explain what we've seen and felt.

This cautious part of my mind was still trying to reason with me, but I was so immersed in my séance that I couldn't listen. I asked again, "Lana, are you here?"

And I'm not sure if it was what I wanted or if Lana herself guided the planchette over the word *Yes*. But this was more than about writing now. I needed to talk to Lana. It almost seemed crazy: a grown man sitting in a basement at two a.m. with a Ouija board calling out to a girl he hadn't seen in over twenty years. It would have been crazy if I weren't so sure I could feel her in the room with me. The same feeling that I had when I saw her sitting in the corner etching out slivers of her desk with a ballpoint pen.

Don't ask foolish questions. Avoid questions such as, "When am I going to die?" If the board answers, "In six months," you might just worry about it needlessly.

God, that's a freaky thought. Shouting some creepy question out into the darkness. The hairs on my neck were standing up now. This was more than I bargained for. I was inviting something into my house and I wasn't even sure it was Lana. I said, "Lana, this was just research for my book. I'm trying to write about evil and the occult. I didn't even think of contacting you." That seemed like a jerk thing to say, so I added, "I didn't think of contacting anyone. I've never talked to a dead person. You're the first dead person I've ever talked to. And I only wanted to talk to a dead person to really understand evil for my book. But now that you're here, like I said, I should have talked to you earlier. I should have talked to you in high school when I had the chance."

I sat there in the dark and waited. The candle flickered as I stared at it. I hadn't looked at a candle and waited for the supernatural since I was kid sitting in church with my dad. But those candles seemed lifeless. This candle had power. There was something in the room with me. My hands still lay limp on the planchette. I could imagine this force sliding them over letter after letter as she answered my questions. I could imagine all sorts of frightening things crawling around me right now. I'd never felt the supernatural like this before. It felt like some small breeze of darkness was blowing around in the room. I waited for what would happen next. I waited for what Lana or these evil forces would do.

My hands were still.

And quiet.

And lifeless.

They didn't move. I opened my eyes and looked around. There were some boxes with Christmas decorations in one corner of the basement. Our old baby swing was against another wall. There were picture frames and old clothes and broken toys. There was a bunch of junk down here. But there was nothing supernatural. After twenty minutes of waiting for something to happen, I realized my mind was playing tricks on me. The Ouija board worked as well as it was supposed to. It made me believe for a moment that something was actually going on. That was all the inspiration I would need. But Lana wasn't here.

And my mother was still dead.

Close the board. This is an important step. When you're done with your session, slide the planchette to GOODBYE and remove your hands.

Or this would have been an important step if anything actually happened. Since it hadn't, I just picked up my board and blew out the candle. I'd throw it out with tomorrow morning's trash. Rachel would never know.

1

Out of Sight.
Into Mind.

Garbage pickup happens on Fridays at eight a.m. The night before, all my neighbors wheeled their garbage receptacles as well as carried extraneous bags, boxes, and unwanted junk to the front of their driveways. Every Friday the rusted red garbage truck arrives at eight a.m. The garbage men always come — rain, snow, or any other natural disaster will not deter these guys from picking up our waste.

I stood looking out my front window, again in my robe, again holding my coffee cup. My garbage can was out there and the Ouija board was inside of it. It was 7:55. They would be here in a few minutes and whisk the thing away and out of my life. So then why was I standing there, looking out the window, waiting for the thing be carried away like it was one of my kids leaving for college? Why did I have this impulse to walk outside—

(Don't even put on your shoes, the truck will be here before you can get them both on.)

—and dig through pizza boxes, milk cartons, and other sludge until I found my Ouija board? It was cheap and it didn't work. If I really needed another one, I could go back to the Black Cauldron and get it. Still, I was standing in my robe actually debating digging through my own garbage for some satanic toy that I didn't even believe in, when the red truck arrived.

I ran outside. One of the men had grabbed the garbage can; it was seconds away from vanishing into the dump forever when I yelled, "Whoa. Whoa. Stop!"

The garbage man put the can down. It was surely the first time today he'd been yelled at by a man in a robe and slippers. "I'm sorry. I think my wife threw away something important." I couldn't admit to men who spent their days with other people's trash that I needed my Ouija board back. So I blamed my wife. What kind of husband am I? I looked at the garbage man. "Can I check in there real quick?"

"It's your garbage."

I shuffled through trash bags, boxes, Pepsi cans, and other sludge until I found my Ouija board. It felt good to hold it in my hands. I held the Ouija board close—hopefully they couldn't tell what it was—and then told them, "Carry on."

I walked back into the house. I had my Ouija board stuffed under my shirt and then pulled my robe over it to make sure Rachel didn't see it before I got to the basement. "Honey, why'd you go out there?" Rachel called from upstairs.

"Just wanted to make sure they got all of the boxes we put out there," I called up to her. Now I was lying to my wife and hiding garbage under my robe. I didn't want to be sneaking around on my wife at eight a.m., but she seemed worried that

I'd have an affair/join Al Qaeda if I had a Ouija board, and I didn't want her to worry about that either. So I told a white lie for the greater good. I put the Ouija board behind our boxes of Christmas decorations in the basement — this seemed like the safest place.

When I got back upstairs the kids were eating oatmeal. Apparently there wasn't time for eggs and bacon. Seemed like the first time in weeks they weren't eating something fried. I needed to start helping out with breakfast, because if we kept feeding them a daily breakfast of cholesterol and grease, they'd all have heart attacks before prom.

"Good morning," I said and sat at the table with my kids. "How'd everyone sleep?"

"Pretty good," Adam said. "I had a dream I could fly."

Rachel walked into the kitchen and poured herself a bowl of Wheaties.

"Where did you fly to?" she asked.

"Wherever I wanted. I mostly flew through the clouds. And they were soft like pillows. But you know I could also do stuff like jump off cliffs and not fall because whenever I started falling I could just fly instead."

"Sounds like fun. Did you have any dreams, Lucy?"

"I had a nightscare," Lucy said. Yes, that's right, night-scare. Once in the middle of the night I heard Lucy crying and I went into her room. I said, "What's the matter, honey? Did you have a nightmare?" And she said, "Yeah, I had a really bad nightscare." I thought it was so cute that I didn't correct her. Now she tells all of the other kids in the first grade about her nightscares. When they try to correct her, she says, "It's not a nightmare, it's a nightscare. What is a mare anyway?

77

That doesn't make sense." And then they usually back down because she kind of has a point.

"What was your nightscare about?" I asked.

"Creatures," she said.

"What did the creatures look like?" I asked.

"I dunno. They had yellow eyes."

"And green teeth?" Adam asked.

"No."

"Did you see their teeth?"

"No."

"Then how do you know they weren't green?"

"Adam, let your sister tell her story. Go on, honey," Rachel said.

"I don't remember their teeth. I just remember they had yellow eyes."

"What were they doing? Were they hurting you?" Rachel was getting concerned. Lucy had vivid dreams and Rachel hated it. She usually blamed the dreams on whatever I was watching on TV.

"No, they weren't hurting me," she said. "They were crawling all over Daddy."

* * *

Rachel took the kids to school while I did the dishes. As I was scrubbing them clean I understood why she always gave our children bacon and eggs. That stuff slid right off the plate; oatmeal clung like stucco. So I was in the kitchen with a green scrubby pad prying each oat off the bowls. Probably good I was pouring all of my energy into the dishes because my mind was racing over what Lucy just told us.

They were crawling all over Daddy. Lucy looked right at me as she said this. I was drinking my coffee, but the mug felt cold in my hands. Everything in the room felt cold.

"All over Daddy?" Rachel asked.

"Yeah, he was in the basement and there was a candle and they were crawling all over him," she said. Rachel knelt next to Lucy. "Baby, you know there's no such thing as creatures, don't you? They're not real." Rachel brushed a strand of hair off Lucy's face.

"They seemed pretty real to me," Lucy said. She stared at me as if I were the only one who could give her the answers she really wanted. Her eyes were asking, *Were they real, Daddy? Were those creatures real?*

I wanted to pick her up and hug her and tell her everything was okay. Those creatures weren't real. You just had a bad dream. Yes, I used the Ouija board but nothing happened.

But if I told Lucy this, I'd be admitting in front of Rachel that I'd snuck out and used the board last night. I'd cause all sorts of needless panic in my family. And there was no need for that. The reality was Lucy had a bad dream. That's all there was to it.

(Why would she see creatures last night of all nights? And how could she have known about the basement and the candle?)

There were two possible explanations. The first was my daughter was a psychic. She'd never displayed any psychic powers before in the first six years of her life, but last night they magically appeared to make me feel extra guilty this morning. And if Lucy suddenly did have psychic abilities, well that was great news. After school I'd drive her to 7-Eleven so she could tell me the winning Powerball numbers.

The second explanation was that Lucy saw me in the basement. She could have heard something when I walked into the office to get the instructions. She probably sat in bed for a moment, then decided to find me. She looked in the living room and the kitchen and finally she crept to the top of the basement stairs and saw me with a Ouija board on my lap and candlelight bouncing off my face. That had to be a frightening scene for a six-year-old, watching her dad try to commune with the dead. The candlelight would have made the shadows dance all around the room. Why wouldn't she think they were actual creatures? She'd be so frightened she'd run upstairs, jump into bed, and pull the covers over her until she fell asleep. When she woke up she would have assumed the whole thing was a dream because how could any of that have actually happened? Her dad wouldn't have actually done something like that.

Would he?

After school I'd take her out for some ice cream and talk about it. I would tell her the absolute truth. I would say that Daddy was tricked into buying some game and the man who sold it to him said it had to be played in the dark with only a candle. I would tell her the game was just as pretend as Santa Claus and I was tricked into buying it. I'd explain the only reason that I bought the game was to help me write my book. Then as we finished our sundaes I'd sit with her and answer any questions that she had about the paranormal, God, Satan, the supernatural, or anything else.

Because I wouldn't want my daughter to be confused in the way I was when I was six years old. I'd want to be transparent in a way that my father never was with me. He made me sit in that church and figure things out for myself. He made me light those candles and pray to God, and he never told me what to do when I found out it was all a hoax and God wasn't listening. I wouldn't put Lucy through that. I would tell her that God (not to mention angels, demons, and whatever else you lump in there) was something people made up a long, long time ago when they didn't have things like science to explain how the world worked. And I would not let her have fear of or hope in things that were figments of our imagination.

Then again, who was I to preach? I was the one who actually went back for the Ouija board this morning. What was my problem? I needed to stop. I was already on a tightrope by quitting my job and risking everything with my family; I couldn't start chasing ghosts. I wouldn't. Not anymore. I was so upset I said my resolve out loud, "You hear me, figments of my imagination? None of that last night was real. I don't believe anything actually exists. If you want to prove something to me it's going to take a little more than a scary dream by a six-year-old," I said.

And this is when a chair, Lucy's chair to be exact, slid across the kitchen floor so quickly it slapped into the wall and one of its legs snapped off. No one pushed it. No one moved—

(Something moved it, Charlie.)

—it. No one even touched it. I was standing on one side of the room and that chair just slid by itself. It looked like there was a rope around one of the legs and a body builder yanked it so hard it flew across the room and into the wall where one of its legs shattered.

I heard our front door open. Car keys plunked in our

little ceramic bowl and footsteps crept toward me until I saw Rachel appear in the kitchen. She was about to say hi to me until she saw what I was looking at. "Charlie, what did you do to the chair?"

I didn't say anything.

"Charlie?"

I tried to move my mouth, but I couldn't think straight enough to tell Rachel anything. I stared at her, the broken chair, and back at her again, hoping I could say something that would help me make sense of what I just witnessed.

8

The Writing on the Wall
(or in this case, the mirror)

When I taught high school, every morning was the same. I'd wake up instantly feeling the pressure of my job. Not that the pressure was ever overwhelming, nothing about teaching is all that high stress. It's not like if I did a bad job teaching, people would die, or lose hundreds of millions of dollars, or go to jail for the rest of their lives. I often wonder how people who face that sort of daily pressure sleep at night.

I always slept just fine.

When I woke up, I'd stand in the shower and wonder how busy the line to the copy machine would be. As I put soap all over the loofah, I'd try to decide if I should leave five or ten minutes early to give myself enough time to make copies or prep my lesson for the day. But in the month since I'd stopped teaching, I'd already noticed how different every morning felt. Some days I'd wake up and drink coffee so hot it almost burnt my tongue, and then I'd place my fingers on the keyboard and write a moving, thoughtful, gut-wrenching chapter to my novel. Other mornings I woke up and felt inadequate. I'd stand in the shower and wonder if I really had anything all that interesting to say. I'd wonder: *Who am I that people will want to pay to read the words I've written down?*

On this morning I didn't feel any of those things.

I just felt unsettled. I was standing in the shower lost in my thoughts. I wasn't in any hurry to step out of the shower because that would mean facing my book and facing the questions I had about what happened the day before. I didn't understand why that chair flew across the room, and in fact, the only thing I could tell Rachel was, "The thing just snapped."

"Chairs don't usually just snap," Rachel said.

"This one did."

"How?" she asked.

"I was sliding the chair out from the table to sweep up. And then I reached over this chair to pick something up and it snapped." This was a lame story. But it's not like Rachel was really suspecting her husband—a thirty-seven-year-old man —to lie about the chair breaking.

"It never seemed that flimsy before."

"I know."

"Weird," she said.

No, that's not weird. What would be weird is the thing sliding across the room by itself by some paranormal/demonic/alien force and then crashing into the wall. But me leaning over it to pick something up isn't weird at all. Actually, it's quite normal.

This is what I thought. What I said was, "I know, it is weird, isn't it?"

I turned off the shower and stopped replaying the incident

from yesterday. I grabbed a towel and wrapped it around my waist. The truth was, things had gotten beyond weird. There were only two ways to explain what had happened yesterday — either something caused that chair to snap or I was losing my mind.

Rachel was still sleeping as I started taking clothes out of the drawer to get dressed. "Good morning," I said to her as I pulled my T-shirt over my head.

She didn't answer. Normally she'd give me some sort of cutesy answer when I greeted her, but she was too tired this morning. I went into the bathroom and took out my razor and my shaving cream. I started putting the shaving cream on my face. There was still the steam from my shower lingering in the bathroom. When I looked on our bathroom mirror, it was covered in steam. Only someone had written something on the mirror. It said:

Good Morning Charlie

I looked back in the room, and Rachel was still there in her nightgown lying under the covers. There was no way Rachel could have written this. She would have had to have jumped out of bed, written the message, crawled back under the covers — and then pretend to be asleep. That would be more frightening than if some ghost had written this for me.

"Babe?"

"What, Charlie?"

"Are you still asleep?"

"I'm trying to be."

"I mean, have you gotten out of bed recently?"

"What are you asking me, Charlie?"

I looked back at the mirror. Already the steam was clearing

away. Many of the letters were no longer legible. When I looked back at mirror it now looked more like it read:

Go d orn g C ar ie

I could have let Rachel just roll back over and fall asleep. But I needed a second opinion on all of this. If we lived in a haunted house Rachel needed to know about it too. "Can you come here and look at this?"

"It's perfectly natural. It happens to all guys."

"No, it's nothing like that. Just come here."

Rachel rolled out of bed and walked into the bathroom. She cleared the sleep out of her eyes and looked around. "What am I supposed to be looking at, Charlie?"

"The mirror. Do you see that?"

I could still make out letters like "G" and "d" and "n" and "C," but the steam was clearing up and they weren't as legible as thirty seconds ago.

"I see a mirror."

"Do you see the letters in the mirror?"

"Um ..."

"There's like a *G* and *d*. And that right there, that's a *C*. Don't you see that *C*?"

"Yeah, I guess that could be a *C*," Rachel said. She was still half asleep.

"Isn't that weird?"

"No, that is *kind* of weird," she said in a tone that told me she wasn't listening at all. It was sort of like when I'd be watching a football game in overtime and she'd be telling me this story of marital troubles a friend of hers was having. I'd try to feign concern because I knew she was concerned, but I didn't really care. I just wanted to go back to the game. She didn't care about the magical letters that had appeared in the mirror. She just wanted to go back to sleep.

"There were a lot more letters like a minute ago. There was actually an entire message."

"What did the message say?"

"Good Morning Charlie."

"It said 'Good Morning Charlie'?"

"Yes."

"On the mirror?"

"Yes."

"And you didn't put it there?"

"No. Did you?"

"Me? No."

"Doesn't that creep you out a bit?"

"That someone is wishing you a good morning? Um, no."

"But since we didn't write it. And surely the kids ..."

"You're probably just seeing things, honey. You're burning the candle at both ends with this book and you're not getting enough sleep. Come on, let's go lie down for a few more minutes until the kids get up." Rachel left the bathroom and pulled the covers over her. But I kept staring at the mirror. The letters were gone. All I saw was my blurred reflection.

* * *

After the shower I was in the office and I opened my email. I'd sent the chapters I'd written after the reflection in the TV and the chapter I'd written yesterday after the chair snapped to my writers group. In the first email I opened, one writer told me, "This is freaking scary." Okay, so not exactly a glowing review from *Publishers Weekly* or the *New York Times,* but when you're an out-of-work teacher who spends most of his day in a bathrobe, this is the kind of praise that puffs wind into your writing sails. In the next email a writer said, "You've really got something special here. Can't wait to see what happens next." And this was from a writer who'd had thirteen self-published novels. Those emails changed everything for me. These guys were trashing me a couple of weeks ago and now they loved everything. And it was because of the inspiration I was finding—

(Creating even?)

—in my house. So what if I didn't understand what was going on? I needed to embrace it and keep spurring it on. I needed more snapping chairs, Ouija boards, writing in the mirror, and reflections of stalkers on my TV. Without these, I had a bad book. With all of this (whatever it was), I could actually be crafting a bestseller. Wasn't that the important thing?

Filled with a brand-new flash of inspiration, I opened my manuscript. I started writing and my fingers were dancing across the keyboard. The writing was coming easily again today. And what happened with the writing on the mirror gave me the perfect idea as to what could happen in the third house. I was inspired both by my basement and by the message in the mirror to write the next chapters. Here is what I wrote in the outline for *Progressive Evil*:

> The dinner party progresses to the third house. This home, like all of the others, appears normal enough. In the living room are potted plants, a couch and a love seat tattooed with a floral print, and an old wooden piano.

But James and Kelly don't spend much time in the living room. As soon as they arrive the host says, "Follow me." They are led to the downstairs. The host says, "If you wouldn't mind, stay down here while we prepare the next course for you."

The host pushes the couple into the basement and slams the door shut. Kelly, in her evening gown, runs up to the door and pounds on it. Her pearl necklace sways back and forth as she screams, "We've done everything you want. Just give us our children back!"

There is no answer. Either no one was listening or they were all leaning up against the door snickering at her terror. Neither thought was a comfort.

"We're stuck. We just need to ride this out," James says and then sits on a group of boxes marked "Books."

Kelly leans against the wall, angry with her husband for being so passive. How can he just sit there? Time passes and they don't say a word to each other. There's nothing to say, and besides, through the course of the evening they've grown distant. Conflict brings most couples together, but it's tearing the Davises apart.

Then a message appears on the concrete floor. It looks like an omnipotent finger is carving it as each letter appears on the floor. When the message is finally written it reads, "Why didn't you tell him you didn't want to move?"

What just caused that? they wonder. How is this happening? How is this writing appearing from out of nowhere? James was not only wondering how this was happening though. He wanted to know if there was any merit to it. He looked at his wife and asked her: Is this the truth? Kelly admits she didn't want to move. An argument begins, but the couple goes silent as another question is carved into the floor. It involves a question James had about an instructor at the gym who always seemed to have an interest in Kelly. The new carving causes more fear and more accusations. As they're locked in this basement they're forced to face one question after another about their past, their fears, and their secrets. And the whole time they're trying to figure out how this is happening. Who's causing this?

For another two weeks I worked on writing these chapters. And when I was writing, when I was lost in the story, it seemed like there was nothing paranormal going on. This story was getting good. It was really gaining momentum, and all it took was a few instances of unexplained phenomena. These experiences helped me see the world in a way I'd never seen it before. This made me think of my neighbor's living room and that painting of Jesus with the firefighter. I could picture Blake's words: *The thought of Jesus there with me to provide me strength and courage helps me through things.* Was it possible that some other supernatural presence (I mean probably not Satan himself; I don't know if he can multitask and be everywhere like Jesus allegedly can) was in the office leaning over my shoulder and inspiring me? Sure, when I was seven I decided if I couldn't see it, it wasn't there. But what do seven-year-olds know? I had lots of preconceived notions when I was seven. And my experience changed those notions. I think much differently now about sex, career, family, and life overall than I did when I was a child. So why have I clung so strongly to the notion that I understand how the supernatural works? How could I deny everything I had seen since we'd moved?

I needed to talk about this with someone. I'd tried talking with Rachel, but she either thought I was crazy or she was just downright bored with the possibility of a paranormal event happening on our bathroom mirror. Adam would just shout about how cool it was that ghosts were in our house. That left Lucy.

I'd tried to talk to her over the last couple of weeks, since she'd had the dream, but she never wanted to talk about it. I'd say, "Do you want to tell me about your dream?"

And she'd say, "I already told you."

I'd say, "Are you having any other dreams?"

She'd say, "No."

It went on like this for another week. But finally I needed to know what she'd really seen. Nothing had happened in the last week and maybe Lucy could provide me some insight. I tap danced around the thing before, but today I decided to press the issue. Lucy was in the living room coloring and watching *SpongeBob SquarePants*; this was how she unwound after school. It was the construction worker equivalent of sitting back and cracking open a cold one after a hard day of work.

I sat on the couch and she said, "Hi Daddy," not looking up from her work.

"Hey sweetie," I said. Apparently, she was doing more than just coloring. She had a map of America and she was shading every state with a different colored pencil. "How was school today?"

"Fine," she said and then switched from a light blue to an orange pencil to color the state of Texas. But *fine* was a shorter answer than I was used to from Lucy. Normally she'd tell me about the gossip on the playground or some interesting fact she'd learned at school. But in the weeks since she'd had the nightmare we hadn't talked much.

"Lucy, can I ask you a question?"

"Sure."

"Can you tell me a little bit more about your nightscare the other night?"

"I don't really want to talk about it."

"Sometimes it makes us feel better to talk about things," I said.

"Okay."

"So tell me about your nightscare."

"With the creatures?"

"Yeah, with the creatures."

"Well, it was scary. They were crawling all over you," she said.

"Did you actually see me in the basement? Or did you just dream that you saw me?"

"I just dreamed it. Why? Were there really creatures crawling over you in the basement?"

"No."

"Oh," she said. And then, "I told some of the kids at school about my nightscare. And they said they used to have nightscares too. But then they just started thinking about being a princess and wearing dresses and dancing in castles with princes before they went to sleep. And now that's what they dream about. So I'm going to do that when I go to bed so that's what I dream about."

My daughter was so solution oriented. She just saw an answer and suddenly everything was clear. Maybe I was just being overly sensitive. She wasn't upset with me; she was just doing homework and watching *SpongeBob*. That's all there was to it. Part of me wanted to press her more, wanted to see if she really did have a psychic dream. But what sort of father would that make me? She found a solution to her nightmares and I needed to let her have it. I couldn't drag my daughter into this. Whatever was happening to me, I was going to have to walk through it alone.

9

Cupid's Delight

In those weeks when I was writing about the third house, I expected something frightening to happen. I expected to see creepy twins in pastel blue dresses standing in my hallway and smiling at me. I was ready to look out the window and see a black cat with bright yellow eyes, stinking of the grave and walking across my lawn. Or at the very least I'd open the fridge to make an omelet, and eggs would levitate out of the carton and crack themselves into the frying pan.

I had gone from a skeptic to a believer.

Maybe *believer* was too strong. But at the very least I was open to the possibility that there actually was something supernatural happening inside my house. The three instances —the Ouija board, the chair, and the mirror—made me reconsider my thoughts on the paranormal. At first the question was *if* something was going to happen, now it was only a question of *when*. As I finished the third house in my book, I waited for the next apparition.

But it never came.

No flying eggs or dead cats or creepy twins. No levitating furniture. No ghosts appearing in the mirror. There was absolutely nothing. You might ask *Isn't it a good thing to have a house where creepy stuff doesn't happen at the breakfast table and when you walk out of the shower?* No. I needed something to happen if I was going to finish my book.

And if nothing was going to happen on its own I'd have to force things to happen. This is how I once again ended up at the Black Cauldron in the middle of the afternoon. That same clerk was there (still looking more barista than Goth) and judging me as I wandered around the store. I once again had no idea what I was looking for—I was the tourist looking for trinkets that could invite spirits into my home. That clerk was sitting on a stool behind the counter and reading a tattered Neil Gaiman paperback, or at least he was acting like he was reading while he watched me. He knew I didn't belong here and he was silently mocking my indecisiveness. Every other person who walked into his store must have had in mind the perfect cultic item that they needed to commune with Satan or whatever it was people did with this stuff.

Finally, I found something called *The Book of Everyday Spells*. This seemed like the type of item that could inspire me while not giving my daughter any nightscares. I picked the book up, and after reading the back cover, the book was exactly what it sounded like: a book of spells to help a person out in their everyday life. None of the spells were that impressive. The spells didn't make fire appear out of a magic wand or ghosts show up in the middle of a person's living room. They were all more tame things like helping a person find good fortune or love or parking spaces. I placed the book on the counter and took out my wallet. As the clerk rung it up I asked, "Are there some good spells in here?"

"What do you mean by *good*?" he asked. Every sentence he spoke was dripping with judgmental subtext. I wondered if it was just me or if he treated all of his customers like this.

"I mean, are there some helpful spells in there?"

"We don't call them spells."

"What do we call them?"

"We call *it* magic."

"Really, just magic?" I asked.

"Yes."

"Isn't magic kind of what the guy with the top hat does at a five-year-old's birthday party?"

"Can I get you anything else, sir?"

"Just the book of magic spells," I said.

* * *

Yes, I'm thirty-seven years old and I was about to try casting magic spells. Frankly, I feel embarrassed every time I think about it. There was a reason J. K. Rowling made Harry Potter twelve years old when the series started out. Because it's cute when a twelve-year-old says "Caperinous-Contornous" and causes a candelabrum to float. But if Harry Potter had been middle aged when the series started it would have been downright embarrassing.

And that was me.

A middle-aged Harry Potter.

The Book of Everyday Spells had two different sections, one called "modern spells" as well as what it called "classic spells." There were lots to choose from. There were spells that would curse my enemies. The modern spells would give them the flu—while the more classic spells would give my enemies the bubonic plague. I didn't want to cast any of these types of spells. I didn't know if I really wanted to cast any spells at all. For the first couple of days I was just reading the book in my office, the living room, and in bed at night before I fell to sleep. I was looking for the right spell to cast, which should have been easy, but the spells were intimidating. I thought it would just be chanting a few words, but none of them were that simple. Every spell required specific props, the perfect environment, and the right frame of mind for it to work. The book was very clear on that. It's as much about the person casting the spell as it is about the spell itself. It was like Satan, or the queen of Wiccan powers, or whomever it is that makes magic work wanted to test you. And to me it seemed like a lot of work, as if I could be putting myself out there and nothing would happen. So I decided if I was going to cast a spell it needed to be the right spell.

I couldn't pick the right spell.

Rachel picked one for me.

I was lying in bed reading my book of spells and she was next to me with her glasses on reading *Julie and Julia*. She was a bit obsessive in her own right (this is why we were such a great couple), and this memoir was inspiring Rachel to bake and then blog about it. Rachel's passion was desserts, so she began to post about macaroons, chocolate soufflés, vanilla cupcakes with fluffy white frosting—she'd snap pictures and then she'd write about it. Other people would comment on the dessert we just ate, which to me felt a little invasive. It was one thing to use our lives as inspiration for novels, quite another to write and take pictures about the dessert we just ate. But we didn't have a lot of friends in Castle Rock and the dessert blog made her happy. Rachel seemed deep into thinking about the next dessert she was going to bake when she pulled down *Julie and Julia* and asked, "How's your book?"

"It's fine, I'm not really reading it for fun. It's more for research."

"Do you believe in them?"

"In what? In magic spells?"

"Yeah, in magic spells."

"I don't know. Do you?" I asked.

"Not really. But I guess it's possible. I mean, a lot of people believe in that stuff. Maybe there's something to it."

"Want to try one?" I asked her.

"No, that's not a good idea," she said.

"What, are you scared?"

"No, it's just not a good idea."

"Come on. It will be fun. If it works it'll be cool to watch. If not, no big deal."

"Fine, but I get to choose the one we try," she said. If she was pushed hard enough she couldn't say no. I think that's how I ended up getting her to marry me, and I know that's how we ended up here.

She put *Julie and Julia* down and began thumbing through the spell book. "What about this one?" she said and showed me a page in the book. The spell she'd stopped on was called *Cupid's Delight*, and it was a spell that would cause two people to fall in love. Only my wife could turn my quest to understand darkness into a romantic comedy.

"Is there someone you want to fall in love with you?" I asked.

"Not for me."

"Who for, then?"

"For Dave Myers and Jenny Williams," she said in a tone of voice that implied I should know who these people were.

"Dave ..."

"... and Jenny. You know Dave and Jenny. I see them at the mailbox nearly every day. How have you never seen them there?"

"I don't get the mail that often," I said. Our rental home was in a suburban development with a community mailbox. This was the most communal place in the neighborhood, which is why Rachel usually checked the mail.

"They're always out there and they talk forever. Sometimes they'll be out there by the mailbox for at least half an hour. That's how everyone knows who they are."

"Gotchya," I said.

"Jenny really has a thing for him. She laughs at everything he says. That's like the number one way you can tell when a girl likes a guy. When she laughs at things that aren't even funny."

"You used to laugh at my jokes."

"I must have really liked you."

"So we're going to cast a spell on them," Rachel said as giddy as a junior high girl.

"Sure," I said.

The next day we were around the corner from the mailbox, just out of eyesight. Rachel had the book of spells, and I stood right next to her holding a red candle. This reminded me of the basement and the Ouija board and the yellow candle, and I had the same feelings of doubt that were there on that night. The instructions in the "Cupid's Delight" chapter told us to be somewhere romantic, preferably outside. At least we were outside. I did not think the mailbox was particularly romantic, but Rachel said there couldn't be a more romantic place because this is where their romance first sparked.

Once Dave and Jenny were in the depths of conversation and flirting, I lit the red candle while Rachel whispered the following chant, "Love here. Love now. Love all around." She chanted this over and over while I held the lit candle. Finally, I took a red rose we bought at Super Target and sprinkled petals onto the ground. We were out there for a total of five minutes. It felt like an hour. Rachel chanted a prayer for our neighbors to fall in love. I was praying that no one saw us.

Once the spell was cast we sneaked back home as if we were a couple of teenagers who just toilet papered our volleyball coach's home at midnight. Of course it wasn't midnight. It was three in the afternoon, and there were people all around the neighborhood raking leaves and teaching their kids to ride their bikes. Rachel and I said brief hellos to everyone, but we tried not to get trapped in a conversation. We didn't want anyone to ask why we were walking through the neighborhood with a candle, a broken rose, and a book of spells. We didn't want anyone thinking we were the neighborhood witches.*

---

*Not that I thought there was necessarily anything wrong with being the neighborhood witch back then. I just didn't know the first thing about witching. If someone came to me with a question or problems that only a witch could answer, like, "How do I ride a broom?" I would have just stood there dumbfounded.

Rachel slammed the door shut and we both let out a sigh of relief. We locked eyes with each other and smiled. "Do you think it will work?"

"I don't know," I said.

"What if they do fall in love? What if they get married? Do you think we should tell them we cast a spell on them and we're the reason they got married?"

Rachel ran over to the front window and peeked through the shades. I peeked in behind her and we watched as Dave held his mail and unlocked his door. "Just think of him in that big empty house. Alone. Every day. I hope our spell works," Rachel said right before Dave walked inside his home and vanished from our watching gaze.

10

White Magic

I wrote these chapters where Jim and Kelly were strapped into chairs with leather cuffs and chains. The chairs were similar to something an inmate would be strapped into right before lethal injection, only Jim and Kelly were strapped in so the hosts could cast spells at them. At first, the spells forced Jim and Kelly to fall in love. But then that wasn't very interesting, so I had the hosts cast spells so the couple fell *out* of love. Also not very interesting, so then I had the hosts cast a spell on Jim and Kelly to give them the bubonic plague, which then made my heroes very sick and they just wanted to lie around. It's hard to fight back when you have the bubonic plague. I ended up throwing all those chapters in my digital garbage bin. And I learned one very important lesson.

Spells are not scary.

I spent an entire week on those chapters only to find out that spells have no place in a horror novel. I learned that spells were essentially positive thinking with props. How could I create a bone-tingling scene with positive thinking? Magical spells have a place in fantasy like Lord of the Rings or Harry Potter, but spells and elves and the power of positive thinking have no place in a horror novel.

I needed to move away from spells and find something frightening to inject into my home so I could get an idea for my next scenes. Rachel, however, was not writing a horror novel so she wasn't quite as willing to brush spell casting aside. In fact, a couple of days after we cast our first spell Rachel burst into my office and said, "Dave asked Jenny out."

"Wow. That's great."

"Great? That's it?" she asked.

"No. It's really great."

"It's more than really great, Charlie. This means our spell worked."

"Well, it doesn't necessarily mean it worked."

"How can you say that?"

"What if it's just a coincidence?"

"It's not just a coincidence—"

"Rachel, these are two people who clearly liked each other. Isn't it inevitable that he would ask her out?"

"There is nothing inevitable about it, Charlie. People like each other all the time and they miss each other. This is what's so tragic about love. Sometimes it takes something more than *just liking each other*; sometimes it takes a push by fate, or destiny, or *magic*."

Overnight, spell casting became her new hobby. She cast spells for our Adam to get the lead role in the elementary school's production of *Aladdin*; spells for better parking places; spells for more money to come in. And Rachel felt that her spells were working. Adam got the role of Abu the monkey. I told Rachel, "It's not even the lead role." And she said, "Yeah, but Abu really is the most important and lovable character in *Aladdin*." She found a twenty-dollar bill in her jacket *out of nowhere*, and we did seem to get an unprecedented string of good parking spots.

Rachel was astonished by every one of these acts of magic. It was hard for me to be that impressed. I'd seen real paranormal events, or at least things that were real enough that it would take more than a twenty-dollar bill to astonish me. Still, there could be a use for Rachel to become so fascinated with casting spells. For these final chapters I needed a truly frightening event to happen in our house. I needed a few mind-bending twists to propel my book toward greatness. That meant I needed more than levitating furniture and friendly notes in the mirror. It was going to be hard enough to create these sorts of events, but they'd be nearly impossible if I had to sneak around like a teenager anytime I tried to dabble in the paranormal. I needed Rachel's buy-in. I needed her to want to go along on this journey with me. And maybe casting spells could be a gateway to get her to follow me into some more useful activities.

But I didn't want to push her too hard because everything so far—moving, quitting my job, the debt we were racking up, the friends we'd left behind—was already a strain on our marriage. I had to wait until the right moment to bridge the subject. That right moment came out of a dinner we had with Blake and Tammy.

We invited them over to reciprocate for the lasagna meal they made for us. Things started out innocently enough.

Sure, we didn't have any Jesus paintings for décor, but that didn't seem to bother Blake or Tammy. In fact, the subject of religion didn't come up until late in the evening when someone started talking about good luck.

"I don't believe in good luck just happening. I think you have to make your own luck," Rachel said.

"I couldn't agree more. Luck happens to those who work hard and take advantage of every opportunity," Tammy said.

"Well, sure, that. And by thinking positively about what you want to happen," Rachel said.

"Yeah, a good attitude is important," Tammy echoed.

"Well, I believe it's about more than a good attitude. There's a little bit of magic involved."

"Magic ..." Tammy said. "Oh, you're joking. I get it."

"No, I mean not like pulling a rabbit out of a hat, but I think if you want something to happen bad enough you can make it happen if you know the right spells," Rachel replied.

"Wait ... you believe in magic spells?" Tammy asked. She was rattled. She couldn't tell if Rachel was joking or not, but either way, spells were not a subject that you joked around about. Why not just joke about children starving or homelessness?

"Charlie bought me a book of magic." I wasn't sure how I was the one who suddenly bought the book of spells for her. As if all of this positive thinking with props was my idea. "I can't believe how much those spells work," Rachel added.

"You're casting spells?" Blake said.

"Yeah."

"On what?" Blake asked.

"Lots of things. School plays, people, parking spaces," Rachel said.

"Have you cast any spells on us?" Tammy asked.

"No, do you want me to?" Rachel asked.

"NO," Blake and Tammy said. Blake knew they came off a little more startled than he wanted to, so he said, "No, it's okay. We're not really comfortable with spells. We think they're dangerous."

"I'm not casting the dangerous ones."

"Like what?" Tammy asked.

"Voodoo dolls, curses, things like that," Rachel said. I took another bite of meatloaf. This was interesting to watch. We'd never had any close evangelical friends and Rachel hadn't grown up in church. Religion and mysticism were new to her. She had no idea how freaked out Blake and Tammy were. Rachel didn't understand that to them there was no difference between the "good" spells and the "bad" spells. To them it sounded like she was saying, "I'm only using the good cocaine. I'm not using any of the dangerous stuff like crack."

"We think all of the magic is dangerous," Tammy said.

"Really? Why?"

"It's witchcraft," Blake said.

"It's demonic," Tammy added.

"Demonic?" Rachel said. "Isn't that a little melodramatic? I'm not going to the church of Satan."

"It's true. Rachel's never been to the church of Satan," I said.

"It's not like I'm sacrificing pigs or anything. I'm just trying to cast spells that bring money and good luck," Rachel added.

"That's how Satan fools us," Tammy said. "That's how he lures us in. Sure, someone like you isn't going to cast curses or use the really demonic stuff. He's going to get you hooked with the seemingly innocent stuff. They're gateway spells, Rachel. But if you start messing around with that for too long, pretty soon you'll host your own séances, you'll have pentagrams all over your house, and who knows what else."

"What's so evil about a circle around a star anyway? Just seems like a bunch of shapes to me."

"I don't know. All I'm saying is there's always a catch to this stuff. It brings more than you bargained for," Tammy said.

There was a lull at the table. No one knew what to say next. Our conversation, and perhaps our friendship, was at a standstill. "I'm going to get us coffee to drink with our dessert," I said.

I left the table. On my way to the kitchen I stepped into the bathroom and shut the door. I turned on the sink and ran my soapy hands through the hot water. As I dried my hands I looked in the mirror and I didn't like what I saw. No, it wasn't another message. But if it had been, it probably would have said, "Lose some weight, Charlie." I was fifteen pounds overweight. I was slightly balding. Of course slightly balding was how it started. Soon slightly balding would turn into comb-over balding. And then I'd have some real choices to make. Would I let myself go all the way bald until I just had a ring of hair around my head like Friar Tuck? Would I use Rogaine? Did that stuff even work? I hated the thought of losing my hair. I always wanted to have distinguished-looking hair in my forties and fifties like Steve Martin and George Clooney.

But if I wrote a bestselling novel, would it really matter how distinguished my hairline was? Does anyone really care what Dean Koontz or John Grisham's hair looks like? Sure, Tom Wolfe has cool hair, but if he couldn't write nobody would care about it either. I just needed to create the type of book that would put things into perspective. The way I saw it, if you're a bestselling author and you have a receding hairline, no big deal — if you're out of work and you have a combover, well in that case, you're in trouble.

I turned off the faucet. I couldn't think that far ahead. I needed to be in the now, and right now I needed to get out there and join the conversation. This conversation could really help me get Rachel to come to my side of the argument. After all, she didn't want to end up like Blake and Tammy, the witchcraft police. Rachel understood that what she was doing wasn't that bad; in fact, if anything, it was helpful and fun. Was using a Ouija board really that different?

(Prove it to her. Make something happen right now.)

I dried my hands. I wasn't sure where that idea came —

(It doesn't have to be much — just get the kitchen table to float. Something like that will freak out the churchgoers. Rachel will be sucked in by its beauty. She'll have to know more. She'll have to know how this is happening. And then she'll follow you wherever you need her to go.)

But how could I just make something happen? I didn't have my Ouija board nearby and the book of spells was upstairs. What was I supposed to do, go to the basement, grab my Ouija board, slap it on the table, and light some candles? Everyone would think I'd lost my mind.

(Just ask for something to happen. Demand to see something.)

So, in the bathroom while Rachel was entertaining our guests, I meekly asked, "Why don't you just show yourself? Let my wife understand what's happening here. Is that so hard, to show me who you really are? If anything's here make yourself known."

I waited.

I had another moment of belief. I was ready for the lights to flicker out; a shrouded ghostly image could appear in the mirror; maybe I'd walk into the dining room and see that this time my chair had flown across the room and snapped in half. Rachel, Blake, and Tammy would be mid conversation, debating things they didn't understand, and their conversation would screech to a halt as my chair levitated and danced above them. Maybe I'd even step out of the bathroom and see Tammy staring at that chair, and I'd say, "That's even scarier than a pentagram, isn't it?"

But nothing happened in the bathroom. When I walked into the dining room, neither the chair, the dessert, our cats, nor the children were levitating either. "I thought you were getting coffee," Rachel said.

"Sorry."

"I'll get it," Rachel sighed. She walked to the kitchen and came back with the coffee. She poured us all a cup but no one was really talking now. The room was tense from the debate about magic, and it was clear that we'd all be eating our desserts as quickly as possible so this evening could come to an end. As we were finishing Adam walked in the room with a disposable camera and said, "This looks like a special moment. Can I take a picture of everyone, Mom?"

"Sure, sweetheart," Rachel answered.

We gathered together and posed for the picture. This was the perfect moment for something frightening to happen. And I kept thinking some inspiring demonic manifestation would happen at any moment as Adam said, "Say cheese," and snapped our picture.

The Picture Adam Took

I'm not sure which is more unbelievable: The fact that unexplainable events were happening in our home or the fact that we had a disposable camera. You might be asking—aren't disposable cameras pretty much extinct? And even if they aren't, do children really just walk around with them and take pictures of adults at dinner?

Let me explain.

This wasn't just a disposable camera. This was an underwater disposable camera that we'd bought for Adam on vacation last year. We bought it for him because he saw other teenagers using them, and we feared if we didn't get one he might take our nice camera for a swim. Within the first hour he used up most of the roll snapping pictures of strangers' legs, thighs, and feet. Before long, he'd scared everyone out of the hotel pool. So Rachel told him, "Why don't you just save the rest of the pictures until we get to the beach?"

Adam of course forgot the camera when we got to the

beach and it stayed buried in his suitcase for the rest of the vacation, stored in his room when we got home, and it was packed away in some box when we moved. But on that afternoon when we were cleaning and getting ready for Blake and Tammy to come over, it appeared. I could never get a straight answer of how this camera suddenly showed up. "It was just there," Adam said whenever I interrogated him about it.

Adam started snapping pictures with it as soon as he found it, until Rachel said, "Why don't you save a few of those for tonight?"

"Okay," Adam said.

And then, for reasons that made little sense to me at the time, he determined that a dinner with neighbors we barely knew constituted a "special moment." That photo was the last one on the camera.

I forgot about the picture until a few days later when I was in the office pointlessly working on my story. My writing had dried up ever since all supernatural activity in our house had come to a standstill. I heard the front door shut and Rachel said, "Charlie, can you come here?"

I walked downstairs and Rachel was holding the freshly developed pictures. She handed me the picture from our dinner. In the photo Rachel was smiling, Tammy and Blake looked surprised, and I looked hopeless.

The ghost, however, looked slightly evil.

Yes, the ghost. It was a hazy white mist curling behind me and smiling a smile that said — *I'm here.*

In your home.

I like it here and I've been here a long time.

You can't see me, but I can see you.

114

We all looked so naïve, not even noticing this thing in the picture with us. I instantly thought of the bathroom. I thought of begging to see something and feeling so disappointed when nothing was there. Of course that was the problem. Something *was* there. But it took Adam with his disposable underwater camera to show me something I was too blind to see. Was this the thing that had written the note on the bathroom mirror, that had guided my hands across the Ouija board? Was this the face of the creature that had thrown the chair across the kitchen?

"Tell me I'm not crazy," Rachel said.

"You're not crazy," I echoed.

"You see it too?"

"The ghost?" I said.

"Ghost? You're calling it a ghost?"

"That's the first word that comes to mind. Is there something else that you would call it?" I asked.

"No, I just wanted to hear you say it first."

"Well, I said it. It looks like a ghost to me."

We both paused and looked back at the picture. We wanted to double check to see if we were right. The picture hadn't changed. We all still had those stupid smiles on our faces and that ghost was still hovering above us. Just looking at the picture sent shivers through my backbone. It was like watching the horror movie where you knew the killer was in the closet ready to pounce and there was nothing the poor unsuspecting teenagers could do. Except this time *we* were the poor unsuspecting teenagers. And seeing yourself like this, with a ghost hovering over you, well it's chilling. It's bone chilling. But to me it was also beautiful. It said *not all*

115

hope is lost. It said there still may be a way to find inspiration for your novel.

Rachel finally said, "Could this be some glitch? It's just a cheap camera, right? Maybe it just got overexposed ..."

"This looks like a lot more than a glitch—"

"Well, it's really creepy."

"It's more than creepy. What if it means our house is haunted?

"Charlie, isn't that a little much?"

"No, I think our house might be haunted. And maybe I'm the one who's causing it."

"Really? How?"

"There's something I need to show you."

* * *

We made our way down to the basement, and I was more than ever thinking about the house we'd moved into. What if all of my actions spurned something to life? Was I poking at supernatural forces with a stick just asking to get bitten?

If so, I wasn't like most people. Most people move into houses that are already haunted. Usually there is a death, sometimes even a murder, and after that, instead of going to heaven or hell or hanging out with the other ghosts in the cemetery, the spirits decide that their time is better spent turning faucets on and off in the middle of the night and showing their reflections in the mirror. Sometimes the spirits will make sounds—the poor people in the haunted house will hear scratches on doors, whispers, crashes, and occasionally shrieks of pain and terror. The spirits will do this for a variety of reasons: it could be that their murder remains unsolved, and the spirits want the new residents of the home to find out how they really died. Movies tell us that spirits want justice.* Which makes sense if spirits are dead people because people certainly feel entitled to justice. Of course movies also tell us that some spirits had a miserable, horrible life and want everyone else to be just as miserable.†

My point is this: no matter what the reason for the haunting, people usually move into houses that are already haunted. People usually don't bring the haunting on themselves.

I'm not most people.

Most people scream when doors click shut and look around like frightened puppies when the lights suddenly flicker off. But I was *controlling* how my house got haunted. Nothing happened unless I asked for it to happen. I was the one who asked for the ghost to show itself, just like I asked for everything else to happen. Now I could bring Rachel in on what was happening here and it would open so many more possibilities. Most paranormal games were meant for at least two people, and now with Rachel alongside me we could really push to see some spectacular things.

Rachel and I were standing in the basement amidst our boxes. She looked at me, wondering why I'd brought her down

---

*See *The Sixth Sense, The Others, The Frighteners,* and *The Lovely Bones* to get a better understanding of the "I want someone to know what really happened" hauntings. You can usually tell where the plot is going without even turning on the movie just because the word *The* is in the title.

†See *The Haunting, The Amityville Horror, The Shining,* and *Poltergeist* to get an understanding of the "misery loves company" hauntings. Of course three out of four of these titles also have the word *The* in them. Kind of shoots my previous theory to pieces. Maybe if the word *The* is in the title, then it has a high likelihood to be a haunted house story. I'm going to have to do more research and come back to this later.

here. That's when I pulled apart the two boxes of Christmas items and showed her my board.

"What is this?"

"It's the Ouija board I bought."

"Have you been using it?"

"Just once."

"When?"

"A couple of weeks ago?"

"What happened?"

"Nothing happened. Or I thought nothing happened. But then remember that chair that broke in the dining room? Well, it didn't just break. Something pulled it across the floor and made it break."

"Something pulled it?"

"Yes, and then I saw that writing in the mirror in the bathroom. And then last night I asked to see if something was really in our house. That's when this ghost appeared in our picture. Something is happening here, Rachel."

"Why do you sound happy about that?" Rachel asked.

"Because I think I'm making it happen."

"Charlie, are you okay?"

"Listen, I'm coming clean with you. You asked me to throw the board away and I didn't. And that was wrong. I don't think using it was necessarily wrong, but sneaking around you was. That's why I'm bringing you down here. I want you to go on this journey with me."

"Charlie, I'm going back upstairs."

"Okay, I know this is a big request. But I need you. This is for our future. Things are happening, and this is helping me write the book like you wouldn't believe. I mean, you saw how flat it was. And you've read it lately. You've seen how much better it's gotten, haven't you?"

"Casting spells is one thing, but using a Ouija board—"

"It's not that different. Okay, to Tammy Bates it's different, but she assumes all of this is evil. But it seems to me like I'm writing a great novel and our kid is getting the best part in the school play because of this *evil.*" I was convincing myself with my speech to Rachel. Really, what had I done that was so bad? What really is *evil*? Is it just a label? Who decides what's good and what's evil? Churches? Politicians? The Parent Teacher Association? Are these really the people that make the decisions? And why are we so willing to believe them?

"How can you compare some good-luck spells to a Ouija board?"

"Because they're not that different. They're both just tools. I know if you were Tammy and Blake it'd be hard to have an open mind about this. But you've seen how those spells work; now I'm just asking you to have an open mind about the next step," I said.

"How am I supposed to do that?"

"Let's use this together," I said. I was holding up the Ouija board. "Let's see if something really happens. I used it once and maybe something happened. Maybe it didn't. But I was all alone. I don't want to be alone. I don't want to sneak off and do this by myself anymore. But the more I can see, the more it inspires me. So, please, let's use this. If it gets uncomfortable we'll throw it away. If nothing happens we'll still throw it away. If something happens we can talk about it. I just don't want to do this without you anymore. So I'm asking, Rachel, will you help me?"

12

Late Morning Ouija

It was 11:30 and I was in the basement hanging blankets over the windows. We couldn't let any sunlight in for our séance, and I didn't want to wait another day for Rachel to go along with me. The iron was hot and it was time to strike. Rachel just watched me with her arms crossed as I duct taped different quilts and packing blankets over the windows.

"Sunlight adds interference. Just trying to keep all of that out so we can have a good séance," I smiled.

"Sure," she said. But I could see she was thinking something like *That's kind of weird, Charlie. This is all a little strange. What have you been doing down here? You've turned from my heroic husband who was bravely crafting a novel into the Wicked Witch of the West.*

Or at least I assumed she was thinking something like this because she wouldn't talk to me. She was just shifting her feet and looking all around. I said, "Are you okay?"

She said, "Yeah," but kept looking around nervous as a

shoplifter. I laid the Ouija board on the blanket next to our vanilla cupcake candle.

"That's the candle you use?" Rachel asked.

"It's supposed to be white. White symbolizes good."

"What does vanilla symbolize, Betty Crocker?"

"All right, I'm new at this. It was the closest we had," I said.

"What do we do now?"

"We have to choose someone to talk with," I said. This I decided was the hardest part of any séance. If you choose someone you care about (like your mother or friends who've passed away in high school) it makes the séance far too emotional. If you choose a celebrity/historical figure, you have no way of knowing if what they are saying is the truth.

"Why don't we talk to whoever slid the chair," Rachel said. Her tone was shifting. Maybe I'd misread her. She wasn't scared; she was just annoyed at this whole thing and didn't believe my story.

"I don't even know if that was a person."

"Only one way to find out," Rachel said.

"You realize I said I *think* our house is haunted. I said I think something's going on here and it's helping my writing. Not that I absolutely know everything. Just that maybe something's happening."

"Well, let's see if something's happening," Rachel said and flicked off the lights in the basement.

I looked at my wife for a moment more and then lit the yellow candle. *What was this? She was acting like I was the one on trial?* "You need to put your hands on the planchette," I told her.

"What's the planchette?" she asked. I motioned to the heart-shaped piece of wood on the board. "Okay," she said.

"Close your eyes," I said. Rachel obeyed. With our eyes clinched shut I said, "To whomever slid my chair ..."

" ... and wrote a good morning message to Charlie in the mirror," Rachel added.

"Yes, to whoever you are, we're calling out to you. Are you here?"

There was nothing for a moment. It was this horrible pregnant pause, where it seemed that we could be so let down. Where I was sure nothing would happen, and Rachel would look at me like a fool for thinking I had seen things. If I was on trial I was about to be found guilty. It'd be such a letdown that it'd call everything into question. The direction of our lives, our marriage, our home, everything was in the hands of this ten-dollar board from Parker Brothers.

Again I asked the empty room, "Whoever you are, we know you're here. We've even seen you in a picture."

We opened our eyes. A slight gust of wind was whirling through the basement. The candle flickered violently. And then out of nowhere our hands were moving.

"Are you doing that?"

"No," I said. "I don't think so." Our hands continued to move until the planchette landed on the word "YES."

"It said yes. What does that mean?" Rachel asked. There was a laugh and a bounce of excitement in her voice.

"I think it means he's here," I said.

"You don't know it's a he," Rachel said.

"He or she is here."

We looked all around to see if there was anything in the room. Nothing in the basement but ordinary things. No hovering vapor or mist or anything supernatural the naked eye could see.

Rachel shut her eyes again and asked, "Why are you here? Are you trying to communicate with us?"

Again it took a moment for our hands to move and then the planchette slid back to the word "YES." Rachel looked up at me. Her eyes sparkled like a child's. "You didn't move your hands that time either?" she asked me.

I shook my head no.

Rachel asked, "Then what are you trying to say?"

Our hands began to slide again. First they slid over the "I," then "N," then "E," then "E," then "D."

I NEED. He's (or she if you ask Rachel) was saying I NEED something. But I NEED what? I NEED help, I NEED you, I NEED souls to feed on? It took forever to say something on the Ouija board. And this is when I realized I needed to know what this ghost—

(How are you so sure it's just one ghost?)

—was trying to tell us. Yes, I wanted inspiration for this book, but it was more than that now. I couldn't just type THE END on my manuscript and forget that all of this ever happened.

Next our fingers slid over to the letter "H." What could "H" possibly mean? Was it for "help"? Or is the ghost a husband looking for his long-lost wife Harriet? Or maybe a wife looking for her long-lost husband Harry? Did our hands slide over the "H" on accident? It was right next to the "K"; maybe our ghost meant "K."

Click.

The door above the basement clicked open.

"Mommy, Daddy, what are you doing?" It was Lucy. Her eyes were sharp, as if Rachel and I were the ones on trial now. I could see it dawning on her little first-grade face that something wasn't right down here. That she'd walked in and seen something children aren't meant to see.

"Baby, what are you doing?" Rachel asked.

"It was only a half day today," Lucy said. Adam had walked her home from the bus stop, which meant he was upstairs rummaging around for a snack. But as soon as he found one he'd be down here too. This was not the place Rachel and I wanted our kids to find us. We backed away from the Ouija board. The candle still flickered—

(Is that ghost still down here? Is Lucy going to have another nightmare?)

—off our faces. I felt dirty having Lucy see us like this.

"Nothing, honey," I said. "It's just an old thing we found." I grabbed the board and blew out the candle. I was trying to be as unspecific as I could. If I called it a game she'd want to play. If I said, *Mommy and Daddy are trying to communicate with the dead*, she'd be very afraid of her parents.

"Come on upstairs, honey. I'll make you a snack."

* * *

That night Rachel and I lay in bed. The kids were always around so that whole day we hadn't talked about what happened with the Ouija board. We didn't even know what was going on. How could we talk about this around them? What were we supposed to say? "Adam, Lucy, don't be alarmed, but our house might be haunted. So if you see your stuffed animals floating around in the middle of the night, don't worry, it's completely normal." It seemed irresponsible to expose our kids to that kind of fear. In fact, I was beginning to wonder if there was any way to keep chasing these ghosts or supernatural apparitions or whatever you wanted to call them while still being a responsible parent.

I was there in the dark with these thoughts dancing through my mind. I thought we might go to sleep without talking about it. But I finally broke the silence and asked Rachel, "Do you think Lucy saw anything?"

"I don't know. She seemed fine. She probably just thought we were acting a little strange. Adults act a little strange sometimes."

"Yeah, I guess so," I said.

"Charlie, I think you're right." Rachel was rapidly switching subjects. I guess Lucy wasn't her biggest concern.

"Right about what?"

"I think there's actually something going on in our house."

"I'm sorry. I didn't mean for it to happen. I was just trying to research —"

"No, I mean I don't think that's bad. I think it's pretty amazing that something's going on here. I never believed in ghosts."

"Neither did I."

"But something happened in our basement. Didn't it?"

"Yeah. Something was there."

Rachel didn't say anything for a moment. It was like she was just sitting in the dark considering the weight of everything she'd seen so far. Finally, she said, "Charlie, I think our house might be haunted. And I think we should find out just how haunted it really is."

13

Clowns
in the Casket

Rachel decided we should approach demonic encounters as if we were baking. This meant we could no longer just take out a Ouija board, light a candle, or call out to the dead and see what happened. First, there would be thinking, planning, and organizing. We needed ingredients (the tools and props necessary for pulling off a séance) and we needed a recipe (the plan on how to pull off the séance).

Rachel also needed a goal. When she baked, she needed to know how her cupcakes stacked up to everyone else's and was just as curious about what other people did to make their desserts unique. One blogger might say, "I know this recipe called for blackberries, but I used raspberries" and another might comment, "I used a caramel drizzle instead of a chocolate drizzle." It was this sort of maverick disregard for the recipe that Rachel admired most. Yes, there was a way to bake this dessert, but if you were going to make it from scratch, why not make it perfectly for your family?

And if we were going to pursue the paranormal, why not pursue it perfectly for our needs? Rachel thought if we really understood the history, the culture, and the traditions around the paranormal it would make my writing all the more vibrant. Thus far I had just been trying to *experience* things, but if Rachel could help me research, then I should be able to write the type of scenes and characters that bestsellers are made of. I couldn't believe how passionate she'd become. A few weeks before she was telling me to throw away the Ouija board; now she was pushing me to go deeper into this than I would have ever gone by myself.

This was a twist that I did not see coming.

Rachel began her research — she already had a start because she knew about spell casting blogs and websites. She'd be on her laptop researching while I started my chapters about the fourth house of the progressive dinner. Sometimes as I was writing, she'd say, "Charlie, come here."

She'd usually discovered a new site or video on YouTube. "Look at that." It'd be a picture of a bunch of senior citizens in a hot tub, smiling at the camera, while a skull was carved into the steam over them. The caption underneath the photo said, "You're all going to die soon." "Creepy, huh?" Rachel smiled.

"Yeah, it is creepy," I said. The image disturbed me, but it seemed Rachel thought it was just *icky* in a fun Scooby Doo way. Before long Rachel was knee-deep in a subculture complete with books, memoirs, podcasts, TV shows, blogs, and hundreds of websites. On a lot of the sites there were places where users could upload their own photos of ghosts and apparitions. And the caption under every photo said something to the effect of, "I promise that no Photoshop or other manipulation was used on this photo. It just came out like this when it was developed."

Everyone uploading these photos was begging to be believed. This longing to have our fears validated might be one reason people love horror movies and novels so much. It's as if the horror story says, *It's okay. You should be afraid.*

After a couple of days in this world, Rachel found the things we needed for our ghost hunt. And when she'd finally completed her list, she sent Adam and me to Walmart while she and Lucy cooked dinner.

Adam and I looked through the list of everything we needed: a stopwatch, flashlight, thermometer, lantern, digital voice recorder, digital camera, first-aid kit, headphones, microphone, a journal, and a pack of ballpoint pens. Rachel said these were most of the items we'd need for our own homemade ghost hunting kit. I was glad Adam was there because he knew what was state of the art. An eight-year-old boy has a much better grasp of technology than a middle-aged English teacher/novelist without a job. Adam told me, "These are much better headphones," or he'd point and say, "No, not that camera. This camera!" As I was loading up the cart he asked, "Dad, what are you going to use all of this stuff for?"

"Well, it's kind of for a science experiment," I said. I was looking at digital voice recorders at the moment. I had no idea which one would be best for ghost hunting.

"I love science experiments. Can I help?"

"No, this is more of a grown-up science experiment," I said. Adam scowled. He was eight years old. He'd be in junior high in just a few years. I was learning I had to be careful about what I said around him. Who knows what he was thinking when I said "grown-up science experiment." I tried to clarify, "It just might be dangerous."

Adam looked at me with his sad eight-year-old eyes. The excuse wasn't working. And as I looked at my son, I thought maybe I could just bring him along. Maybe he could help Rachel and I out. He had a better handle on all of this equipment than I did, so he could show me what to do if something wasn't working right.

I know you're probably thinking I'm the least responsible dad in the world. I know you're probably thinking it's one thing to get your wife involved in ghost hunting, but now you're pulling your eight-year-old son into this. I can understand your logic.

But here's the thing:

My father taught me how to be respectful and well liked by others. He was completely honest and forthcoming when he taught me about money, about sex, and about how to be successful in business. But my father never talked to me about God, angels, demons, or the afterlife. He dragged me to church to light candles and pray for Mom. But he never explained anything. Never explained what prayer was, or how church worked, or why there were all of these creepy old paintings on the wall and weird images in stained glass. He explained the birds and the bees but it was up to me to figure out the supernatural and the afterlife. I didn't want to make the same mistake my father made with me. So shouldn't I tell Adam what I was doing? It wasn't really that dangerous, was it? And wouldn't he rather know instead of waking up in the middle of the night to discover his dad wandering around the house with a digital voice recorder and a microphone? Maybe the safest thing would be to just explain to Adam what we were doing. Maybe we could explain it to Lucy too. We'd be *The Walkers— Ghost Hunting Family.* I bet we'd have a reality show made about us in six months.

"I'm not scared, Dad. Let me help you," Adam said. He could tell I was thinking things over. He had this instinct of when to close the deal. He was going to go far in life.

And I might have said yes, but I couldn't. Not yet. Not until I really understood what I was doing. "Adam, I have to try this first, but if it's safe, I promise I'll bring you along."

* * *

We read bedtime stories to Lucy, tucked the kids in, and kissed them goodnight. We decided it was safest not to start ghost hunting until the kids were asleep so they didn't walk in on us again.

We watched TV for a while and then I went upstairs. Adam and Lucy were out. The coast was finally clear. I took the ghost hunting tools out of the plastic Walmart bags and placed them around our wood-paneled living room to assemble everything. I didn't realize how much there was. Before I knew it our couch, love seat, shag carpet, and recliner had been overtaken by batteries, boxes, and sealed plastic bags with different parts of digital gadgets. It felt like Christmas Eve when Rachel and I would stay up through the middle of the night assembling bikes for Adam and Lucy to open on Christmas morning.

As we finished Rachel said, "So what are we going to do?"

"I thought you were the one with the plan," I said.

"My plan was to get all of this stuff so we could capture evidence of what was going on here. The websites say every home is different. And you're the expert at getting something to happen," she said.

"Okay, sure, you're right. Well, I've been thinking about this. Every time I've genuinely addressed this ghost, demon, whatever you want to call it—"

"Don't call it a demon."

"Why not?"

"Demons are gross. *Ghost* sounds like it could be friendly. So does *spirit*. But *demon*, I don't know, that word freaks me out."

"Okay, so then we'll call it Casper."

"Great," she said.

"So my thought is, we just call out to Casper." I took the Ouija board out of its box and started setting up. "I'll use the board and you can take pictu—"

"Let's call out to it now," Rachel smiled. This was not like her. We had a recipe for what we were trying to do.

"You want to call out to it now?"

"Yeah."

"We don't have everything ready," I said. I hadn't even put batteries in our digital camera.

She wasn't even listening. She grabbed my hand, clutched it tightly, and said, "Can you show us a sign?"

"Rachel, come on. Just wait a couple more—"

"I want to see it. I want to see you. Whatever you are in our house, you've teased us long enough. We want to see what you really are." Like usual, nothing happened right away. But this time that wasn't good enough for Rachel. This time Rachel wanted results, so she said, "It's not that big of a deal. Just show yourself to us. Unless you're scared. Are you scared of us?"

My wife was actually taunting the spirits in our house. I could feel a chill in the room. My arm hairs stood up. My spine tingled. The room must have gotten ten degrees colder. Something was happening here. But Rachel kept pushing for more.

"You're the ghost. Aren't you the one who's supposed to be doing the scaring? Well, we're right here."

"Rachel, don't make the ghosts angry."

"I'm not angering them. I just want to see them."

"Maybe you should ask more nicely."

"Why? Isn't this our house? Aren't we the ones paying rent? I'm pretty sure these ghosts aren't paying anything—"

"We just don't know what they're going to do if we upset them," I said.

"What are they going to do? Break furniture?" Rachel turned and looked at the walls and ceiling. "Please, break our furniture. I'd love to see that." We both instinctively looked at the coffee table. I'm not sure why, it just seemed like the most logical thing that the ghosts would break at that moment. I think we both collectively pictured the thing lifting in the air and then the ghosts—

(Demons. *Wasn't that really the word I was looking for? Didn't that word sound more accurate? Didn't ghosts just seem like a euphemism for demons? I told Rachel and Adam that we didn't know if they were evil or not. And maybe I didn't. But if I'm honest with myself, I think in that moment I knew better. I knew whatever we were hunting and waking up wasn't a friendly, shy little creature. It was nasty and thirsty for destruction and it didn't want to just say hi to us or tell us about the future. It wanted something more. It wanted—)*

—throwing the table down and letting it snap in half. Of course the ghosts didn't break our coffee table. They aren't pets. They aren't circus monkeys. They're not going to perform for you. You're not going to get ghosts to do anything you want them to do just to show off. Even back then I knew that.

"Fine, if you won't break our coffee table, then why won't you—"

THWACK. THWACK. THWACK.

This was the sound we heard. I don't know how to type it other than to write *THWACK*. But I can tell you this—it was loud and it was angry. It was telling Rachel to shut up. It was telling us *Here I am. You wanted to see me, well here I am. I'm not going to just show myself to you, but I'm a lot closer than you think.* It sounded like a creature with the strength of a bulldozer was pounding against our living room walls. The walls shook on those three hits. It was a minor earthquake in the Walker house. But Adam and Lucy didn't wake up. Maybe whatever we were hearing was meant for our ears only.

I scrambled over and picked up the digital recorder and microphone. I wanted to record these sounds. I wanted to play them back and make sense of what I was hearing. I could even take it to an expert to analyze later. I held the microphone against the wall. And then I heard it. It sounded like scratching.

Like fingernails clawing against wood.

Like someone was trying to claw out of a casket.

I looked at Rachel. She looked back at me with a face that said, *Yeah, I hear it too.* We looked back at the walls. It was just one or two pairs of hands scratching at first. But then it was more. It sounded like a graveyard full of hands coming to life.

And then there was laughing.

It sounded like a clown was laughing at us from behind the wood paneling. The laughing had a kind of diabolical joy that usually belonged to comic book villains. And just like the clawing at our wood, there was only one voice laughing at first. But then more chimed in; clowns were laughing and clawing at our walls.

I dropped the microphone and Rachel stood next to me. I held her tight. It was all I could do. We were as helpless as frightened teenagers in a slasher movie. We were a husband and wife who foolishly thought we understood what we were doing. Now we were going to have to pay the price.

Then Rachel pulled away from me. She crept up to the wall and placed her palm against it. Her eyes lit up like a child looking at a creature in the zoo for the first time. She slid her palm up the wood paneling as if she could actually feel whatever was on the other side.

(Pull your hand away. They can feel you touching that wall. And there's not just one of them. We thought there was just one of them. But we were wrong. We've been wrong about everything, and if you don't get your hand off that, these clowns, these creatures, these demons, are going to rip through that paneling and take you with them. They will drag you away screaming. And you'll just stand there, won't you, Charlie? You'll stand there frozen like when

you saw that murderer in the TV reflection. You'll just stand there because you never know how to save anyone.)

"Rachel, what are you doing?"

"Can you hear that, Charlie? It's pretty amazing."

"Rachel, get away from the wall."

Rachel turned away from me and turned her focus back to the laughing and the clawing. This was my fault. I'd convinced Rachel to follow me into this—I'd begged to do it. We'd chased it together. And now for the first time I wanted it to stop. I had no idea how to make that happen. I hadn't read far enough in the ghost hunting manuals to know how to reverse it. This was like spelunking. We'd walked into a cave with some equipment because it sounded fun, but we were in too deep and we didn't know how to get out.

"Rachel," I said again. She didn't turn back; she had both hands on the wall now. She was looking at it as if she could see right through it into—

(Are you seeing something? Are you hearing something? What is happening to you, baby? Why won't you talk to me?)

—another place.

I took a deep breath.

I closed my eyes.

The clawing and the laughter grew louder. It was so loud now that I couldn't think. And I pictured Blake's painting of Jesus and the firefighters. He was holding that hose and giving them the strength to overcome the fire. This was an awkward thing to see at a moment like this. But I wasn't thinking that. I wasn't thinking how lame it was to have a picture of Jesus helping out firefighters in your living room. All I was thinking when I saw Jesus was that maybe he could help me.

I didn't believe in him, but when you're faced with this kind of evil in your house, your living room, when you feel this kind of evil closing in on your wife, it makes you rethink things. And so with that picture of Jesus holding a fire hose in my thoughts, I whispered, "Please—"

The clawing was so loud now I couldn't think. It sounded like something was about to break down our walls. If I didn't do something right then I wouldn't be able to do anything again. So this time I shouted, "PLEASE, make them stop."

Silence.

Everything went away.

Our living room was still.

No more laughter. No more clawing. It was like waking up from a bad dream. My plea to the son of God holding a fire hose worked so well that if I hadn't seen that look on Rachel's face I might have thought I'd imagined the sounds of laughing clowns and clawing on my living room walls.

14

Intense and Undeniable

Our living room was a disaster. Walmart bags with half-opened equipment, digital cameras without batteries, unlit candles, a Ouija board on the floor with the planchette still in the box. I glanced at my reflection and saw I looked just as frazzled. My skin was a pasty oatmeal color and it looked like my first grey hairs had arrived. The room was quiet though. The clowns had stopped laughing and there were no claw marks to prove that they'd ever been here. But I could feel their residue.

"We should clean all of this up," I said.

"It can wait," Rachel countered and went upstairs.

"We can't just leave all of this."

"Come on, let's go to bed," she called back. "I'll help you put it all away tomorrow."

What? Tomorrow? This could not wait until morning. I didn't want Lucy seeing all of this and I didn't want to remind Adam that we'd done something here. Adam would say, *How'd it go, Dad? Can I help next time?*

And I'd reply, *No, son, you can't because we invited a VW Bug's worth of demonic clowns into our living room and they nearly tore the place apart. So you won't be helping next time. You will never be near any of this again.*

I cleaned everything up. I carried the equipment down to the basement. I put our inflatable snowman over the Ouija board; I covered the recording devices with strands of Christmas lights. When I got back upstairs Rachel had changed into her nightgown. She was as beautiful as the day I married her, maybe more so, her hair wild and her eyes untamed. "Hi Charlie," she said in a tone she used only when she was trying to be extra sultry.

(Are you actually finding all of this attractive?)

"Rachel, we need to talk," I said.

"Yeah, that was pretty amazing," she said.

"It was frightening."

"Well, of course it was frightening. It gave me chills."

"You're not acting frightened."

"What am I acting like?"

"Like you're just soaking it all in. You look like a star-struck teenager more than someone who was shaken by this experience. And to me that's almost as frightening."

"Well, I'm not trying to act like anything. I mean, it was scary, but it was also amazing. I think I had my first paranormal encounter tonight. And it was an intense, undeniable encounter. Most people go their whole lives without ever witnessing something like what we just saw."

"Yeah, I mean sure, but we don't know what that was. That didn't sound like Casper out there. That didn't sound like anything friendly. Those things wanted to—"

"We don't know what they wanted to do."

"It sounded evil, Rachel."

"Well, maybe I just made them mad. Maybe I pushed them too hard."

"Yeah, and they could have—"

"But they didn't do anything. You told them to stop and they stopped. You're in control of this whole thing," Rachel said. "I believe in you. I believe in everything you've done so far. And I just want to help you see it through. Okay?"

"Thank you, honey," I said.

"Now let's get some sleep."

But I couldn't sleep. Every time I closed my eyes I heard the covers rustle and thought it was something clawing at our walls, or I heard Rachel breathe and thought it was laughing in the distance. I turned on my side, stared at the wall, and turned my thoughts to *Progressive Evil.* Then it came to me. What if the fourth house was alive? Hadn't this book been about the personality of every house? Well, what if in the final house Jim and Kelly are locked into, the house is some living, breathing thing? It laughs at them, claws at them— it's so alive it nearly drives them mad.

I got out of bed to write. I couldn't sleep so I needed to do something. I started crafting chapters about the fourth house. When I looked up from my laptop I could see the sun rising in the east. Before long sunlight covered the walls of my office and melted away the night. I rubbed my eyes and took a drink of water. I was so tired. I couldn't keep this up much longer, but I was so close now. Rachel was right; all I had to do was stay in control.

15

Charlie's Angel

I buried myself in the office for the next week to finish the chapters on the fourth house. Every time I came out of the office I'd see Adam and Lucy fighting about TV or chores, and soon the kids were arguing about everything. Rachel always looked exasperated at the thought of making another meal. It was the same over and over—something to eat for breakfast, lunch, and dinner—it never ended. She was in cooking purgatory. She used to find solace in the kitchen but she hadn't baked for weeks. I never left the office, and in turn it seemed my wife and children decided not to go out either. We were a family of four and we'd all come down with cabin fever. We were spreading the germs of isolation, boredom, and claustrophobia on the furniture, dishes, and everywhere else in our outdated rental home.

I didn't want my family to suffer. But we were all part of writing this book. I understood that now. We were running a marathon and the final miles are where it burns the most.

When this was all over I'd take us on a vacation and we'd laugh and spin on the teacups by day, and at night we'd talk about how much we loved each other as we watched fireworks light up the Magic Kingdom sky.

We were so close to the end. I just had to write the final home. This was Jim and Kelly's home. When they left for dinner that night they thought they were just going to have the neighbors over for dessert. And now they had no idea what was going to happen.

The problem was, neither did I.

Rachel and I hadn't done anything with the Ouija board and the ghost hunting equipment since the night of the laughter and the clawing. That night seemed far away now. At the time it was too much; I thought I was losing my mind; I thought creatures actually were going to rip through my house and walk into my living room. Now it didn't seem that bad. I just needed my next demonic fix so I could write my final chapters with confidence.

I was in my office putting the final touches on the fourth house and thought maybe tonight I could talk Rachel into doing something. Not sure what yet, but I had the whole day to think about it. I shut my laptop and went to the shower as I started to wonder what we should do. What sort of event did I need to happen in the finale?

I was still in my bathrobe. I stumbled into the bathroom, opened the shower door, and twisted the hot water knob. Nothing came out. There was no pressure on the valve. It just twisted with no resistance.

"Charlie," Rachel yelled from downstairs.

"Yeah," I yelled back.

"The water in the kitchen isn't working," she said.

Great. Just what I needed.

I turned on every water faucet in the house. The bathroom sinks, the kids' bathtub, the kitchen, the shower again, anything to see if I could get water coming out. Nothing happened. I called the utility company and they said the water should be working. They gave me a plumber to call and when I dialed him he said he'd be there in an hour.

"Did he say it'd be expensive?" Rachel said.

"Didn't ask."

"You should have asked."

"Do you want to call and ask?"

"No. Whatever," she said. "Lucy and I are going to mommy/daughter play group. Do you want to stay here and write and wait for the plumber?"

"Sure," I said. This was the last thing I needed. An uneventful morning with a plumber while my deadline was inching closer and closer.

* * *

Rachel began going to mommy/daughter playgroup about a month after we moved. These were the only new friends she had in Castle Rock and she'd just gotten to know them over the last six weeks. She wasn't close enough to them that they would invite her to their surprise parties and BBQs, but Rachel still loved every Saturday morning. It was the get-out-of-our-old-outdated-house card and she needed someone to talk to besides our neighbors. Mommy playgroup was her escape.

It always went the same. The host mother and daughter

made enough tea and scones for the mommies and the daughters. Then the daughters would go down to the den and laugh and dance like six-year-olds while the mothers sat around the living room drinking tea and eating scones. The conversation revolved around exactly what you'd expect. If you don't know what to expect, imagine a group of women talking about reality television, the trials of parenthood, and the complex dance known as marital intimacy. These are the normal subjects. Demonic activity is never a talking point for the mommy/daughter playgroup.

That's why this mommy/daughter playgroup would turn out to be so memorable. Rachel was upstairs with the other women sitting on a couch overloaded with throw pillows, while Vicki, the host, was pouring everyone tea and making sure every cup had ample sugar and cream. While she poured she asked, "What do you ladies do for fun with your husbands?"

"You mean besides ..." Marcy asked.

"Yes, besides that," Vicki said and blushed.

"Well, that's good because that's not very much fun anyway," Marcy said.

Everyone laughed.

Marcy was like the resident Joy Behar* at the playgroup. She always pushed the jokes a little too far and all of the other women loved her for it. Rachel wondered how the other

---

*Joy Behar is one of the ladies on the daytime television show *The View*. I have a theory that *The View* is subtly one of the most influential shows in television history. When other women get together in settings like this they think they must interact like the women on *The View*. So they have to ask themselves: Am I going to be the mentor, the intellect, the wacky liberal, or the perky Republican? Where do I fit in?

women looked at her. If she had her choice she would be the Barbara Walters — wise, traveled, intellectual, and compassionate. The other women would look up to her for all of her experience, but Rachel would still fit in like she was just one of the ladies.

"No, I'm talking about hobbies," Vicki said. "Do you have any hobbies with your husbands for fun?"

One mommy said, "Derrick and I like to go snorkeling every time we go to the Cayman Islands."

"When was the last time you went to the Cayman Islands?"

"Seven years ago."

"Oh," Vicki said and put her teapot down. The seven-years admission was a little deflating. "Anyone else have hobbies with your husbands?"

Other mommies chimed in:

"Jim and I used to go to wine tastings. We even had a wine cellar. But now it's filled with old baby toys and boxes of clothes."

"Kyle and I played tennis when we were first married."

"We used to go camping, but now it's just too much of a hassle. You just feel dirty and you have to put your Oreos in plastic bags so bears don't eat them," Marcy said. And then there was silence. All of the mommies were a little horrified to realize they had no hobbies with their husbands.

Rachel took a sip of tea and blurted, "Charlie and I just started ghost hunting." Every woman turned and looked at her with reverence and fear and respect. It was the same way the women on *The View* looked at Barbara Walters.

"You have to tell us about that," Vicki said.

I was up in the office when the doorbell rang.

"Dad, the plumber's here," Adam said.

I went downstairs to greet the plumber. When I picture a plumber I think of an overweight, slightly balding guy with a mustache who wears his pants unfortunately low. The man Adam let in the house was 6'5" and as chiseled as a European swimsuit model, and his hair was blond and curly. I looked at him and thought I knew him. But from where? Was he a parent of a student? No. I couldn't quite place where I'd met this guy before.

"Thanks for coming over so quickly," I said, shaking his hand.

He said, "I am here to serve," and then shook my hand back. His grip was firm as iron.

"I'm not sure how much they told you about the problem—"

"They told me everything I need to know," the plumber said. "Why don't you show me your bathroom where the problem started."

"Sure," I said. We walked up to the bathroom and he took out his wrench and started messing with the showerhead.

"How much is this going to cost me?" I asked.

He took his wrench away from the showerhead slowly. He stared at me. And in a deadly serious tone he said, "If you don't get this fixed it could cost you everything."

"Um. Okay," I replied. This was not the type of cryptic answer I expected from a plumber. He went back to the shower for a few more moments and then he looked at me and said, "I think I know exactly what your problem is, Charlie."

"Great."

"You've been inviting demons into your house."

I stared at the plumber for a dumbstruck moment. Was this some kind of joke? Who was this guy?

"Excuse me?" I asked.

"Let me say it again. This time a little slower. You've been inviting demons into your house. There is darkness here, Charlie. Normally, darkness just slips into my clients' lives. They don't go flat-out looking for it. Especially not a guy like you. Family man, writer, teacher—what are you doing messing with this stuff, Charlie? Why are you playing with forces you can't possibly understand? I thought you were through with it after you heard all of that laughing, and then this morning you start thinking about more things for you and your wife to do."

"What kind of plumber are you?"

"I'm not a plumber," the plumber said.

"Then who are you? I just need someone to fix my shower."

"Your shower's fine."

"No it's not."

"Yes it is. Try it."

I twisted the knob and the pressure was back. Water started to flow, and within ten seconds it was hot enough to bathe in. I cranked the water back off and looked at the plumber.

"How is that working? You didn't do anything."

"It's working because I made it work."

"But it was broken five minutes ago."

"It stopped working because I needed to get your attention."

149

"Wait, you shut it off? I'm going to have to report you to your boss."

"Charlie, are you really going to make this about water? You know what you've been doing. You've been messing with the Ouija board—"

"That's how I know you."

"How?" the plumber said.

"You were the guy I ran into when I bought my Ouija board."

"Yes," the plumber said.

"Why are you following me? Why are you doing this?"

The plumber didn't say anything.

"Answer me," I demanded.

* * *

"Yes, a chair slid across the floor," Rachel said.

"Like in *Poltergeist?*" Marcy asked.

"Just like in *Poltergeist*," Rachel answered. "Weird stuff has been happening ever since we moved into the house. Charlie thought he found a message written on the bathroom mirror. This mist appeared in a picture." Rachel didn't say that it was a ghost hovering over us at a dinner party. She thought this detail would frighten these ladies from coming over if she invited them for dinner at a later date. "And so we started researching how to do ghost hunting. We bought tape recorders, cameras, microphones, and a bunch of other stuff to see if we could record any proof."

"That's amazing," Marcy said. "How romantic. Ghost hunting together. I can't even get Walter to take me to a dollar movie."

"Yeah, the other night we were ghost hunting late after the kids went to bed." The way Rachel was telling this story you would have thought we went ghost hunting every Tuesday night. But she needed to tell it with an air of authority and expertise. If she said, *We've only tried it one time*, it wouldn't have had the same impact. "And that's when we heard these sounds."

"What kind of sounds?" a mommy asked.

"At first it was like a scratching on wood."

"That's scary," Vicki said.

"It wasn't really at first," Rachel explained. "It was weird, but things didn't get scary until we heard voices."

"What were they saying?"

"They were laughing," Rachel said.

"They were laughing?" another playgroup mommy nearly shouted.

"Yeah."

"What's wrong with laughing?" Vicki said.

"Laughing is always evil," the mommy said.

"Not always," Marcy said.

"When it comes to spirits it's always evil," the mommy said again.

"Are you going to do more ghost hunting? Are you going to find out if the laughing is evil?" Vicki asked Rachel. All of the women in the playgroup looked at my wife. She commanded their complete attention and respect now.

* * *

"I'm your guardian angel," the plumber said.

"And you're a plumber?" I said.

"I'm not actually a plumber. It's just sometimes we dress like this to blend in. And like I said, I needed your attention."

"Do most angels have blue-collar jobs? Are they construction workers and mechanics? Or are there any guardian angel lawyers?"

"You're not going to take this seriously."

"I'm just having a hard time believing that my plumbing breaks and an angel shows up to my house. What's your name?"

"Gabriel," the plumber said.

"Gabriel, as in *the* Gabriel?"

"It's a very common name for us. Calling one of us Gabriel is like calling an Italian guy Pauly or an Irish guy Patrick. Really not that big of a deal," Gabriel said. This was unbelievable. I didn't know if I should call the cops. But I was getting used to seeing the unbelievable and pursuing it to its conclusion. And he was saying a lot that I couldn't ignore. Of course I was fine with everything he was *saying*. The problem was *who* he was pretending to be and *how* he knew everything about me, including my thoughts. "Are you ready to listen to me now?" Gabriel asked.

"Sure."

"I've done everything I can to protect you so far. But I'm not going to be able to fight them off much longer if you keep this up. Next they might get Rachel or the kids."

"My family is fine," I said.

"Rachel hasn't been depressed? The kids aren't fighting?"

"That has nothing to do with ghosts. This is just a stressful time for my family," I said.

"Are you sure that's all it is?"

"Why would the ghosts ever hurt us? I've never done anything to a ghost. I'm pro-ghost. I'm very ghost friendly."

"You think you can use the other side to get some ideas for your book and leave it at that? You can invite them in, but they're not just going to leave once you're finished. You may be done with them, but they won't be done with you."

"So, what do you want me to do?"

"Stop."

"Can I just stop for a certain amount of time? Like could I stop for another week to let some of the haunting leak out of my house, kind of a detox, and then go back to it? I'm really close to the end of my book and I need—"

"These are demons. They don't just leak out," Gabriel scolded.

"Well, you know, I'm saying, maybe they'll get bored. I mean, our house isn't demon friendly. We don't have any toys for them to play with—"

"Charlie, I really think you should take this a little more seriously."

"Really? You do? Because I think I'm being pretty gracious by even having this conversation. You're the fake plumber. How do I know you haven't been spying on me? How do I know you're not just messing with me? I mean, what sort of six-foot-something-tall man dresses up like a plumber and pretends to be an angel?"

"The sort of man that actually is an angel. And this angel is telling you, if you want your family to be safe, you need to stop chasing the dark and you need to find a way to embrace the light."

"Yes, I think we're going to go ghost hunting again tonight," Rachel said. "We just started finding some interesting things. I want to find out more. I'll see if the laughing really is evil. Maybe I'll even bring some evidence to the next playgroup so you can all hear it." The women looked at each other with equal parts excitement and disbelief, like Girl Scouts around a campfire. Rachel took a drink of tea, imagining next group bringing in pictures of actual ghosts. She'd play them the recordings of the clawing and laughing. She'd bring so much evidence it would blow their fragile little mommy minds. And they would respect her.

They all would respect her.

16

I Hope You Learned
Your Wesson

Five minutes after my angel left there was another knock on the door. *Great, now a representative from Satan is here to tell me there's nothing to worry about and to go through with the haunting,* I thought. Or maybe this was someone Gabriel had sent. Was Gabriel really that powerful? Could he send—

(Come on, Charlie. What has he really done? He hasn't appeared out of nowhere. He's just walked into your house and made a bunch of stuff up. Is it really that easy to impress you?)

—someone to just follow up? Life was so much more interesting when you're dabbling with the supernatural. I wish I'd started years ago. I answered the door and it was Blake standing there. Tough to tell if God or Satan had sent him.

"Hey Charlie."

"Hi Blake."

"Plumbing problems this morning?" Blake said.

"Yeah. It's um ... a long story."

"Okay, well I didn't mean to bug you. I was just wondering

if you'd found an extra kid's jacket lying around. We can't find Sam's. We've looked for it everywhere and thought we might have left it here when we were over for dinner."

"I haven't seen one. But honestly, Rachel pays much more attention to that sort of stuff. I'll ask her as soon as she gets home."

"Okay, great. Thanks, Charlie," Blake said and started to leave. *You're going to have to ask him, Charlie. What, did you expect him to just come over and say, "Hey this may be a weird question, but do you need help with your haunted house problem?"* I still wasn't sure I needed help. But the way Gabriel talked about Rachel being depressed and the kids fighting … I mean yes, I was stressed about my novel, but there was more to it than that. Maybe Blake could help me. He could say a little prayer or something to make things better. Even the ghost hunting websites talked about doing things to protect yourself.

"Hey Blake," I said chasing him into the front yard. I was still in my bathrobe. I'd probably had more conversations with this guy in my bathrobe than in actual clothes.

"Yeah."

"This may be a weird question, but do you know anything about praying against ghosts … or um demons … or um Satan?" I was scratching the back of my head as I said this. I was fidgeting because this was so awkward. He thought I was crazy.

"Excuse me?"

"Yeah, well I know how concerned you were when you saw me with the Ouija board. And I said it was just for research. And it was, really; I've never used one of those things in my life. I was just writing a scene about it and so I needed to understand how it worked. But you were right. It was a bad idea. I think I've brought some things into my home that I didn't mean to."

"And you need to cast them out?"

"Sure. Yeah. Cast them out," I said. I assumed Blake was talking about spirits. I knew I'd come to the right place.

"We need to anoint your home with oil," Blake said.

"Sounds great," I said. It actually sounded a little kinky. But whatever—supernatural stuff is weird. I just needed to get used to it.

"Okay, well, there's a prayer team at our church that specializes in stuff like this."

"In anointing things with oil?"

"In casting out spirits."

"Right," I said. "Do you think they can come over?"

"I'll call and see what I can do."

"Thank you, Blake. I just need help. Rachel and I were in our living room and we heard sounds. There was scratching on our walls, voices, laughing—honestly, it was frightening." I put my hand in the pocket of my robe. Providentially, the picture Adam took the other night was in there. "And when you guys were here the other night, Adam took this ..."

I handed Blake the picture. He stared at the image of all of us pretending to smile while there was clearly a ghost or demonic presence behind us.

He looked up at me and said, "I'll call them right now."

***

Apparently, Blake is a man with some pull at his church. Within a half hour there were four people (three women

157

and a man in glasses) at my home ready to pray and slather my home with anointing oil. I say slather because one of the women in the group was holding a Costco-sized bottle of Wesson Cooking Oil and looked ready to grease everything as if my house was a giant baking pan.

"What is that?" I said, looking at the bottle of cooking oil.

"It's anointing oil," a woman on the prayer team said.

"Really? That's it? I thought there'd be like special anointing oil. Like holy oil that was blessed by a priest."

"We don't have priests," the woman said.

No priests and Costco oil? Who were these people? This was a bad idea.

"It's not about the oil," the man in glasses said, "it's about God moving in your home."

"Right," I said. Then I offered them all something to drink but everyone declined. I wondered if they thought my water or coffee would be contaminated with the demonic.

"What's been going on here?" the man with glasses asked me.

"I've been hearing some noises. I saw a chair move in my kitchen. There's just been a lot of weird things going on."

"Tell them everything. Tell them what you told me," Blake prodded. I was letting Blake down by making the haunting seem blander than it was. The prayer group wanted all the frightening details.

"This all started around the time I used a Ouija board about a month ago." They all nodded knowingly at me. It was probably the same look a doctor gives a lung cancer patient who's just admitted to smoking. "I'm a novelist and was just using it for research. But now, I don't know, things have gotten a little out of control—"

"So you're not a believer?"

"In spirits?"

"In Jesus."

"Um, I don't *not* believe in Jesus."

"That's a double negative. I thought writers didn't use double negatives."

"We try not to. I tell my students never to use them. And I try not to use them myself unless they're absolutely necessary like, *I don't not believe in Jesus.*"

"What does that mean?"

"I don't know him personally. But I don't deny him as a possibility either. I'm sort of straddling the Jesus fence. Honestly, I'm straddling the fence on all of this stuff. I didn't believe in it until recently."

"What changed your mind?"

"I've experienced some pretty unbelievable things lately. So now I'm just trying to process what it all means."

The man in glasses stared at me for a long moment. Then he said, "We're going to pray over your home so your family will feel safe. But you won't find peace until you accept some light into your life." I thought he was going to make me read some spiritual literature or say a prayer or something, but it seemed he'd had his say with me. He turned to his team and asked, "Are you ready, ladies?"

"We were born ready," the woman with the giant bottle of oil said.

The prayer team stood up. They all dabbed their hands with Wesson Oil and began to pray. But not in English. It was some weird other language. *Shandlah* seemed to be one of the primary words of this language. In fact, there seemed to be a lot of repeating words. It was more of a chant than a language. "What are they doing?" I asked Blake.

"It's called praying in tongues," he said.

"Gotchya," I said. Christianity seemed much like the occult. Everyone here was like that kid in the Black Cauldron. There was a way things worked and they expected you to know it. If you don't, then you're out of the club. How was I supposed to know what it meant to pray in tongues? Don't all words in some form come from your tongue?

"It's a spiritual language," Blake added. "A prayer language. It's where the Holy Spirit prays directly through us to God."

"That's kind of unusual," I said.

"This coming from the guy who's hearing laughing voices in walls and saw furniture move all by itself."

"Fair enough. All I'm saying is there's a lot of weird stuff going on in my life right now. Just trying to get adjusted to it all," I said.

Within a few minutes the prayer team started to get more intense. They weren't just whispering prayers or chanting in tongues. They were yelling things in English like, "You will leave this house!" One of the women on the team was screaming this at the walls.

"She's kind of intense," I told Blake.

"When you're dealing with demons you have to be very firm," Blake said. And this actually made sense. In my few dealings with the supernatural it seemed like these entities responded to people who knew what they wanted.

A few minutes later everyone was intense. They yelled in English. They chanted in tongues. I held the bottle of Wesson so the prayer team could come and get more as needed. They'd dab their hands and they'd spread oil on the walls. I found myself wondering if oil would stain. Was I going to lose my safety deposit from this prayer meeting? Of course, the house was haunted so maybe I could say it was already like that when we moved in and still get the deposit back.

"Demons and principalities, you have no place here," a woman said.

"Principalities and darkness, you will leave these walls! Leave this furniture! Leave this TV!" the woman next to her shouted. This woman ran up to me, held out her hands, and I poured oil on them. "Thank you," she said.

"Sure," I replied.

"It's going great out there," she added before standing in the middle of the room and shouting, "You will not cause fear, strife, or anger in the Walker home!"

"Father, we pray you wash this home in your light." I got chills as the man in glasses said this. There was a stirring in my living room. I half expected to see creatures peel themselves away from the walls. I didn't see anything. But I was starting to wonder if with the supernatural it wasn't always about what you see.

Adam came downstairs and stood next to me. He walked through all the prayer team in our living room waging war on the demonic. "Dad, what's happening down here?"

"They're praying for our home. Just a little prayer of blessing."

"Demons, you will go back to the fiery furnace of hell where you belong," the woman screamed.

"That's a prayer of blessing?" Adam asked.

"Um, I think so. But let's not tell your mother about this. She might not understand."

"Do you understand what's happening here?"

"I have no idea, son."

"Shandlah, kemosotae," the woman yelled in her prayer tongues.

Her prayer partner was at a no-holds-barred prayer level herself. She screamed, "Demons have no place here! You hear me, demons? You. Have. No. Place. HERE!"

This is about when Rachel walked in.

* * *

"A prayer team?" Rachel said. "Why did you invite a prayer team to our house?" She'd brought me outside because she could never have this sort of argument in front of others.

"Do you not remember what happened last week? Weren't you a little frightened by all of those sounds?"

"It was eerie, but it wasn't frightening. What was going on in there—" my wife said, pointing to our house and referring to the prayer team spreading oil on our walls and yelling at demons, "—that was frightening."

"Come on, Rachel. There was scratching on our walls."

"We were ghost hunting. What, you didn't think there would be a few noises?"

"It was more than a few noises. It sounded like a Volkswagen Bug full of clowns was about to claw through our walls and strangle us."

162

"And then you told them to stop and they stopped. Charlie, we're in control of this thing. It's not that big of a deal."

"I want our family to be safe. I thought these prayers could help protect our home. I mean, what could it hurt?" I wasn't ready to tell her that my plumber/guardian angel led Blake to come over here to anoint our house with oil.

"You're right, Charlie. That's a good idea."

"Thank you," I said.

"If we're going to keep ghost hunting we need to know all of the prayers of protection and how to protect ourselves and our family from any evil spirits," Rachel added.

Wait. What? I thought. But before I could say anything else, Rachel walked inside and started telling the prayer team, "Thank you so much for coming over and praying for our home. Charlie and I are very grateful." Rachel was wearing her best hostess smile. The prayer team smiled back, but they looked drained, as if whatever they encountered here was far more than they bargained for. They probably didn't plan on meeting this much resistance. At least, that was my initial thought. But then as I watched the prayer team pack away their Bibles and bottles of oil I wondered, What if this is a show they put on at every home? What if to feel valuable they always shout in tongues and scream at the walls? Could they really sense something, or were they just acting out to make themselves feel valuable and to make me feel at peace?

Even as I was thinking this, the man in glasses looked right at me. He told Rachel, "You take care of your family." Then he shook my hand and whispered, "Your home is at peace now. I'm not sure what was going on here, but you need to let it go."

163

17

The Shining Knight

Like I said, our home *felt* better. In fact, I don't think I'd been this calm and at peace in the rental home since we'd moved in. I wasn't overwhelmed by dread and anxiety about the novel, the future, or my family's safety. I didn't know prayer could work like this. That it could change the very atmosphere of the place you live. Prayer to me always meant crying out to God for him to change something that could not be changed.

Like your mother's cancer.

Prayer meant wasted energy and wasted time—it was a crutch for those who could not face the realities of life and death. Then there was this prayer. Sure, the methodology was a little unorthodox. Okay, more than a little unorthodox. There was a woman screaming for all darkness and principalities to leave my recliner. I had no idea why darkness and principalities would want to go to a recliner in the first place. But if there was something evil in my home, their prayers seemed to squelch that darkness. I wasn't ready to say that

I believed in God, but I believed in prayer. I believed that as eccentric as that team was, they'd done something here.

Rachel thought that too. She told me so later that day when we were grocery shopping. On Saturday afternoon we shopped for the week's groceries. It was a family affair and all four of us went. Since I'd quit teaching we'd made a new rule — everyone got to decide one meal that we'd eat that week. But each one of us was responsible for whatever meal we chose. That meant we had to get the ingredients, take them to the shopping cart, and then we had to help cook the meal when it was our night. Rachel thought this would teach the kids how to cook for themselves so they'd be prepared when they left home someday.

Lucy always picked spaghetti. I'd say, "Spaghetti? Really, honey? You can have anything in this store." And she'd say, "I know. I want spaghetti." I hoped that in the next few years she'd get more adventurous in her dinner choices. Or if she didn't, I hoped she'd at least marry a guy who liked to cook.

We got to the store and Rachel said, "Okay, everyone has ten minutes to get your groceries. Adam, help your sister out, okay?"

"Fine," Adam said and took off with Lucy.

After the kids left, Rachel smiled at me and said, "Maybe we could put the kids to bed a little early tonight, and you know ..."

"I don't know, actually."

"Do a little more ghost hunting."

"That's not some weird new way for saying you want to ..."

"No!" she laughed.

"You mean you actually want to hunt for ghosts?"

"Yes," she said.

I was the one who needed to go ghost hunting. I was the one stuck with my novel. But I was having second thoughts. A prayer group screamed at demons in my TV and it actually made our house feel better. I couldn't deny something they'd done had helped and now Rachel wanted to—

"Come on, it'll be fun," she said.

I pushed the shopping cart over to the milk aisle. I opened the refrigerator door and grabbed a gallon of two percent. "I'm just a little confused."

"Why?"

"What's in this for you?"

"I just want a few more answers. I want to know what exactly we've really seen. I told the other moms at playgroup..."

"You told the moms at playgroup?"

"They were interested. They thought maybe we should take some more pictures of our ghost and show it to experts. Maybe they'll interview us or write about us in a magazine."

"This isn't a game. Something was wrong last time."

"Fine, you're right," Rachel said. She grabbed the shopping cart and pushed it toward the baking aisle.

"Why would you want to bring it back?" I asked.

She said, "Because we've learned how to control it now—

(She does have a point, doesn't she? You've learned how to tell it to stop and now you've learned how to make your home feel safe. You know how to protect yourself now. Maybe that was the point of today.)

"—it listens to us. I told it to come and it appeared. You asked it to stop and it stopped. And now we know prayers of protection." She grabbed a large bottle of Wesson Cooking Oil. "Apparently this stuff scares ghosts like holy water."

I could see the conviction in her eyes. She wanted this. "Rachel, I think ..."

"I just need a little closure on this, Charlie. I just want to see it all again. It can help you with your book, can't it?"

"I'm really close to finishing. I could use this, but—"

"Then we'll do it one more time. Only this time we'll know how to protect ourselves." She smiled.

I looked at my wife. How could I tell her no? Besides, she was asking for what I really wanted all along.

18

The Five Obvious Ghost Hunting Rules

We worked together to make dinner: Lucy set the table, Adam stirred the sauce, Rachel buttered the garlic bread, and I was in charge of the spaghetti noodles. This was the third time in the last week we'd all cooked dinner together. A few months ago and an hour up the interstate our lives were overloaded with social engagements. Rachel would be working on some party with her girlfriends, Lucy practicing for her next piano recital, and Adam would be at a friend's house playing video games until well after dark. I'm not saying things were perfect now. I'm not saying we sang songs while we tossed dishes back and forth, but living here was bringing us closer. It's like we were in the foxhole together.

Once everything was ready, we sat down to eat.

"I'll say the blessing," Lucy announced. She learned to start praying for things after hanging out with Blake and Tammy's kids. Those kids prayed for everything and told my daughter you should always bless dinner. Praying for dinner was a new tradition for us. Until we met Blake and Tammy I don't think we ever said a prayer before we ate.

In fact, I don't think anyone other than Lucy had prayed in our home before the oil slathering, demonic beatdown prayer meeting earlier that morning.

"Fold your hands and close your eyes," Lucy commanded.

"Why do we have to fold our hands?" Adam asked.

"Because that's the way Jenny prays," Lucy said. Jenny was Blake's oldest daughter and in the second grade. Lucy thought she walked on water.

"It's just the way it's done," I echoed. I had no idea why people folded their hands when they prayed. Was it some symbol of humility, or was it simply a practical way to ensure people didn't fidget with watches and cell phones while they prayed? Soon there'd be a lot more questions about God I didn't know the answers to. So I'd have to tell them the only thing I did know: don't expect him to actually do anything for you. If God is out there he certainly doesn't want us to know. Or at best, he teases us with his existence in cryptic ways like disguising plumbers as angels. In fact, it's so cryptic you're never really sure what you've encountered. Even those cryptic encounters are rare. For the most part, if God is out there, it seems he's fine just sitting back and watching our lives unfold. If you want something that actually interacts with you, try demons.

"Father-God-Jesus-Messiah," Lucy said the mish-mash of names she'd heard Blake utter in his prayers. "I pray that you'd bless our food, I pray that you'd keep our family safe from everything that's scary — "

(She's still having nightscares, isn't she?)

"—and I pray you'd make the spaghetti taste good. Amen."

My family began scooping forkfuls of pasta and a ladle full of sauce onto their plates. I'd lost my—

(from everything that's scary including the creatures, Daddy; please keep the creatures away; they just left—why are you bringing them back? Daddy, please don't bring the creatures back.)

—appetite. Were Rachel and I being that selfish? We were thinking this was just about us, that all we had to do was keep ourselves safe. What was happening to Lucy while we hunted for the supernatural? Maybe this was just as the prayer team described it.

And that's when I saw two creatures.

I had *felt* things before, but I'd never *seen* anything. I could see now. I watched these creatures crawl out from under the table and up Lucy's chair. Rachel drank ice water and smiled at me. Lucy dipped a healthy piece of garlic bread in sauce, oblivious to the demons breathing on her. They looked like she described them in her dream—three feet tall and grey with yellow eyes. They tangled their fingers in her hair. They dangled their arms around her like drunk men at singles bars. One of them pulled its face so close to hers that it could lick her. The other ate a fistful of noodles and stared at me while the blood-red pasta sauce dripped out of its mouth—

"Charlie," Rachel said.

The creatures were gone.

"You all right? You're not eating anything," Rachel said as she twirled pasta onto her fork and scooped it into her mouth. Lucy and Adam were eating just as much, with pasta and

sauce dribbling out of the corners of their lips as if nothing
was wrong at all.

* * *

I pulled the blankets up to Lucy's shoulders and asked, "You
promise you're not having any more nightscares?"

"Yeah, I already told you that," Lucy said.

"Then why did you pray at dinner about staying safe from
something scary?"

"I don't know. I think Jenny prayed that."

"Will you tell me if you start having bad dreams again?"

"Sure, Dad," she said.

"You have sweet dreams, honey," I said.

"Thanks, Daddy."

I shut off the light and left the room. The kids were in bed,
which meant Rachel would want to start the hunting soon.
My doubts were creeping back up. I'd just imagined those
things at dinner, but if that was anywhere near the truth, I
couldn't go through with anything else. I took out my phone
and called Blake. "Hey Charlie," he said.

"Hey. Sorry I'm calling so late; just wanted to say thanks
again for bringing the prayer team over today," I said.

"Glad they helped," Blake said.

"They can't come back, can they?"

"The prayer team?"

"The demons," I said.

"All you need to know, Charlie, is that God is stronger
than the demons," Blake said.

"Thanks again," I said and then I hung up. I wasn't sure
about this answer. I still wasn't sure God existed. But I did

think demons existed and wondered why more people didn't see them. Why weren't they taking over everyone else's lives? Perhaps I was looking at God all wrong. Perhaps God's number one job isn't to help people but just to keep the demons back. Maybe he's like the Hoover Dam for evil, and if he didn't exist, the world would be flooded with darkness. Rachel was probably right. We learned something today, but I needed to put it into practice. I needed for us to have rules for ghost hunting.

This is how horror stories work — the monster exists only to punish people for their bad decisions. No bad decision, no monster. I had to push ahead for my book, but I needed to create a set of rules to keep us on the straight and narrow and to ensure we didn't do anything stupid.

Rules are the backbone of any good horror story.

Gremlins has its three simple rules: 1) Never feed the Gremlin after midnight. 2) Never get them wet. 3) Never let them near sunlight. Vampires are also supposed to stay away from sunlight, but if they get near you, just follow the rules of having garlic, crosses, holy water, and an oak stake to drive through their heart and you'll be safe. In *Ghostbusters* the rule was never to "cross streams" except in that rare emergency when you're facing a Stay Puft Marshmallow Man that's at least fifty stories tall. There are lots of other horror movies with rules. No need to go into all of those — I think you get what I'm saying.

If characters break the rules, they suffer.

And so, taking everything I knew about God and everything I knew about our tendencies, I sat and scribbled down the five obvious rules for hunting the paranormal:

Rule #5 *There's an expiration date.* We were not going to become the neighborhood witches. We were not going to grow overly fascinated with all of this. Once I finished this book we'd shut the door on the paranormal in our lives and this whole experience would simply provide us good stories to tell at an office party, or maybe I could share an anecdote during an interview when someone asked, "Where do you get all of the ideas for your novels?" I'd answer something like, "Well, years ago we lived in a haunted house ..."

Rule #4 *If things get unsafe— stop.* That night with all of the laughter and clawing I should have stopped sooner. I should have stopped the moment I got chills up my spine. I knew how to stop all of this now. I knew how to pray a prayer or how to end the session with a Ouija board. There was no reason to have any spirits or creatures fill us with dread anymore. If things got uncomfortable, we'd simply walk away.

Rule #3 *Don't skimp on the Wesson Cooking Oil.* Not sure why that worked like magic, but I decided every time after we involved ourselves in chasing the paranormal I'd smear that stuff all over. I was going to use Wesson Cooking Oil like a germ freak uses hand sanitizer.

Rule #2 *Only in the house.* There was no need for us to go to séances or haunted mansions or anywhere else on our journey. We could find everything we needed here in the comfort of our own home. I felt in control here, but if we went somewhere else or if we were at the mercy of something else, it might not feel safe. No matter how much Wesson Cooking Oil I had.

Rule #1 *Never involve Adam and Lucy.* This was the number one rule to me. The rule that could never, ever, be broken.

If my wife and I thought that we had to go on this journey, well fine, but we needed to keep our son and daughter out of this. I didn't want them to be frightened, and just as much, I didn't want them to start dabbling in this stuff themselves. I'd come full circle from my thoughts at Walmart. Adam would never help me with ghost hunting. In fact, I hoped he lived his whole life without seeing anything paranormal at all.

19

Slumber Party

Rachel was downstairs surrounded by lit candles and reading a guide to spirits and the paranormal. When I arrived she put down her book. Her eyes were mischievous. She asked, "Are you ready?"

"Almost," I said. "But we need to talk about something first." I told my wife everything I'd been processing. There are reasons people are afraid of ghosts and get worried about the paranormal. I told her that we needed to practice safe ghost hunting. And I decided on five rules that would keep our family safe. I said add any you want to but these are the five I'm thinking of:

> **Rule #5** *There's an expiration date.*
>
> **Rule #4** *If things get unsafe— stop.*
>
> **Rule #3** *Don't skimp on the Wesson Cooking Oil.*
>
> **Rule #2** *Only in the house.*
>
> **Rule #1** *Never involve Adam and Lucy.*

I explained the rationale behind every one of my rules. She nodded in agreement as I unfolded each one. When I finished, Rachel said, "Thank you, Charlie. Thank you for thinking of these and looking out for our family."

"So you agree with all of them?" I asked.

"Absolutely."

"Do you want to add any?"

"No, I think those are great," she said. She was bored with all of this talk of rules. I was like the skydiving instructor going on and on about safety to a bunch of frat boys right before they were going to jump out of an airplane. When Rachel could tell the rule portion of the conversation was over, she said, "Are you ready now?"

"Yes, I'm ready now. What are we going to do?"

"There's a game that I want to play that I was too scared to play when I was a kid ... Bloody Mary."

"You want to play Bloody Mary? What are we, twelve?"

"Charlie, I remember being at a sleepover with a bunch of friends when I was a kid. We were staying up all night and then a bunch of girls decided to play it. They went in the bathroom with a candle and they told me to come with them. This other girl and I were too scared to come. I said it was stupid and I didn't want to see anything, but honestly I was too scared. They all went in the bathroom with candles and I could hear them say 'Bloody Mary.' The first time, they said it and laughed. The second time they were getting scared. By the third time, a girl in the bathroom screamed, 'Please don't do it, I don't want to see it.' But the other girls didn't care. They said 'Bloody Mary' for the third time and all of the girls ran out of the bathroom screaming. And for the rest of the night there was no more giggling, no more talking about what boys we liked the most; everyone seemed too freaked out. One girl woke up throughout the night crying and didn't say anything else until her parents picked her up the next day. Something rattled her, but I've always wondered what it was and if it really works. I've always kind of wondered if something really appears in the mirror. And now we can know, Charlie."

"Okay," I said. I agreed to let her take the lead, and if this was where she wanted to take us, well okay, I guess. But I felt nervous. This seemed like it would be a great story for mommy playgroup but not very useful for creating the climax of my horror novel.

We walked into our guest bathroom with a candle lit. The lights were off and the candle flickered, creating odd shadows and making our own faces appear ghostly. "So, what do we do?" I asked.

"There are a lot of different versions and ways to play* this game. But the most common and universal is to look in the mirror and say the phrase three times."

"Okay. Great."

---

*Rachel was right. There are lots of legends as to who Bloody Mary actually was. In some legends she was a witch that was hung; in others, she was a mother who was wrongly killed; and yet in others, she was Mary I, Queen of England. Which legend you subscribed to dictated how you'd play the game. The most common way to play is the way Rachel and I did, but in some versions a young woman holds a candle up to a mirror while walking up the stairs backwards. The woman will then see the face of her husband after saying "Bloody Mary" three times. But if she sees a skull, that means she'll die before she ever marries. [Source: Theresa Cheung, *The Element Encyclopedia of Ghosts & Hauntings: The Ultimate A-Z of Spirits, Mysteries and the Paranormal* (Lyndhurst, N.J.: Barnes & Noble, Inc., 2006)].

Rachel and I looked at our reflection in the mirror. We looked younger. I'm not sure if it was the candlelight or the atmosphere or what it was, but we looked like twenty-year-olds. Forget skin cream, chasing spirits had taken ten years off our faces. I *felt* ten years younger too. "Do you say it or do I say it—"

"We say it together," Rachel said. "You start saying it and I'll follow."

"All right. Bloo—" I started saying it and then Rachel jumped in "—dy Mary."

"That's one," she said.

"This is stupid. It feels campy. We've seen real stuff, Rachel. Nothing's going to happen."

"Then keep saying it," Rachel said.

"Fine." Rachel and I both said, "Bloody Mary." It was getting real. There was a chill in the room. I knew this was just a game. I knew this was something that junior high girls did at slumber parties, but I was still getting freaked out. Maybe this wasn't such a good idea. I thought of Rule #4: *If things get unsafe—stop.* This was feeling unsafe, wasn't it? But how did I know the difference between what felt unsafe and what was *actually* unsafe? My rules were not as crystal clear as I hoped.

"You're scared, aren't you?"

"No," I said.

"It's okay. I'm scared too. Let's say it one more time," Rachel said. And then without even waiting for me, she said, "Bloody ..." She was saying it slowly and she was clutching on to my arm as we braced ourselves for whatever was about to appear. " ... Mary."

Rachel kept her gaze on the mirror.

180

But I saw something in the hallway outside the bathroom. It was Rachel in her wedding dress. The dress was a pure shimmering white, just like the day we were married. Her skin was pale and young and glowing. Her red hair dangled off her shoulders and her green eyes were as bright as shamrocks. I felt twenty. I was a young groom in a tux burning with anticipation about marrying this creature in front of me. If I could have moved I would have walked out there and wrapped my arms around her and kissed her.

She took her finger and pressed it against her lips. She grinned at me as the skin began to fall off her face. It fell in clumps like meat left out in the sun rotting and falling off a skewer. Soon under Rachel's white wedding dress there was only her skeleton. Her skull smiled at me and said, "I would have never married you if I knew you would do this to me, Charlie."

"I didn't do this to you," I said.

"Well, you're going to pay, Charlie," Rachel's skull said. "You've made me suffer, you've turned me into this you sick freak, and now you're going to pay."

"I'm so sorry, baby. I didn't mean to."

"Didn't mean to what?" Rachel asked.

I turned and looked at my wife standing next to me — slightly older, her hair not quite as red, but with all her skin attached. I looked back to the hallway. Nothing.

"Did you see something?"

"I think I saw something," I said.

"Me too. Wow, that was amazing!" she squealed. She hugged me and kissed me on the lips, the neck, my cheek. "Doesn't all of this kind of turn you on?" she whispered in my ears. No, it didn't. All I could think of was her pulling her face away and her skin rotting and falling off all over again. The thought of my wife wanting to be intimate while her skin was falling off—well, it was all I could do not to lose the spaghetti dinner in front of her.

But that's when I heard, "Mom, Dad, what's the matter?" Adam was standing at the top of the stairs. He looked at us like a concerned parent.

Rule #1: *Never involve Adam and Lucy.* "Nothing, son. Your mother just screamed because she thought she saw a spider."

"Mom, you're such a girl," Adam said. "Most spiders aren't even poisonous."

"I know, honey. I'm sorry for waking you up. Come on, I'll tuck you back in," Rachel said, and she went upstairs with Adam.

20

Cleanse

Rachel had been asleep for nearly an hour. Then there was me, Charlie Walker, in bed with my eyes wide open. I knew the ending to my story. The final twist was so clear now. How had I missed it? Bloody Mary (or skull-faced Rachel) inspired me. But at what price? Something was happening to my wife and daughter. Those weren't just hallucinations I'd had. I was seeing another side of things; I was seeing super-natural torture they were going—

(about to go)

—through. I watched my alarm clock and the time wouldn't change. My head rested on the fluffy pillow but sleep wouldn't overtake me, and even if morning did arrive, I'd be bloodshot and delirious. At least morning would make things okay.

The clock read 1:13.

How long had it been on 1:13? Would it please change? I needed it to change. I needed to get past this night and to morning because the demons couldn't do anything in the daytime. Could they? At least things seemed harmless in the daytime. But right now they could be in Lucy's room and she'd think it was just a nightmare, but the creatures would be actually in there crawling all over her and—

Do something, Charlie.

I threw the covers off, put on my robe, slid on my slippers, and crept downstairs. I took the bottle of Wesson Oil out of the pantry. Could oil really push away those creatures from Lucy? Could it stop my wife's skin from falling off?

I dabbed my fingers with oil and began to spread it across Lucy's doorframe. Then I smeared it across our walls. I prayed as I did it. It was the first prayer I'd prayed since I was seven years old and staring at that candle asking God to heal my mother. I couldn't bring myself to pray out loud. But I formed the words of the prayers in my thoughts, just like I did when I was a child.

I'm sorry if we did something we shouldn't have. If I shouldn't have used that board, or taken pictures of the ghost, or called out to Bloody Mary. I'm sorry we pursued this at all. I didn't know. I didn't know this would happen. I put everything on the line for this book because I had to make it work. But I didn't want to write a good book at the cost of my family. I wasn't pursuing darkness; I was just looking for plot twists. Whatever this is here, please don't let it hurt my family. Please don't let any harm come to Adam. Please keep Lucy's dreams pure. Please keep Rachel's soul safe. Please don't let those prayers that were prayed over our home today count for nothing. Have mercy on us and keep us safe.

Keep us safe.

Keep my family safe.

21

Night Out

"We should join them, James. What they have here is so beautiful and I want to be a part of it," Kelly said.

I felt sick as I wrote this. How could Kelly actually say that to James? The neighbors trapped them. This group of evil suburbanites put them through hell, locked them in basements, and forced them into their demented games. Did she actually forget these freaks kidnapped their children? That somewhere they were locked away and who knows what they were putting their kids through?

Kelly couldn't see any of that. What she did see was that she moved across the country against her will. What she understood was that she left everything behind for James. And now she was here with these people and they had something. They had purpose, they had life, they had community—it was all so attractive. But that was just at the surface, I realized. It was darker than that for Kelly. She actually liked it. She liked the demented games. She wanted to know how something was writing words on the basement floor. And she wanted to inflict all of this on the next couple. They had paid their rite of passage and it was their turn to watch another couple squirm.

As I wrote I thought about Rachel in that wedding dress. I would have never thought of that twist without my vision of Rachel swallowed by evil in that hallway. But when I saw that, I realized it was the worst thing that could happen to James. It's one thing to have forces of evil and your neighborhood against you. But evil in your own home —

(I'm going to make you pay. You turned me into this.)

— in your own bed, that was so much more frightening than any demon or monster or writing on the wall could ever be. I wrote these chapters and I knew the story was good. I knew I was writing something special; if ever I was going to create a bestseller, this was it. I woke up the morning after we played Bloody Mary and wrote the next chapters. I was consumed with writing for most of the week. I created the scenes with the dessert at the final home and Kelly's decision to join them. I didn't know how James was going to respond to this, but I didn't need any inspiration from Ouija boards or anything else to write those scenes. James would think of something. And if he didn't, his wife would fall into the darkness forever.

When I'd finished writing I went downstairs that night and uncovered the Ouija board from behind the Christmas decorations. I tossed it into a cardboard box. I grabbed other things — the voice recorder, the notebooks, the camera — I just wanted our home purged of anything connected with the darkness. I took the box and threw it in our garbage bin amidst the trash bags and spoiled food. The next morning I watched as the garbage men came and picked it up. This time I didn't run out and stop them. This time I stood in front of my living room window, sipped my coffee, and grinned as the truck drove that board down the street and out of my life.

Rachel stood next to me, and as I watched the truck drive away I looked at her and said, "I'm nearly finished. I've finished all of the parts that I needed to research."

"I'm glad to hear that, baby. I'm proud of you."

I took another drink of coffee. "I threw the Ouija board away. I threw everything else away too."

"You did?" she said.

"I should have told you first, but I just wanted to get it all out of here."

"I understand," she said.

She understood.

I cannot tell you what a relief it was to hear her say she understood. She didn't really care about the Ouija board. She wasn't Kelly. I wasn't living out my novel. This was real life and evil hadn't taken her over. She was the woman I loved and my book was nearly done and things were better now. "I want to take you out and celebrate. Let's pick a time this weekend."

"Can I pick the place?" she asked.

"Anywhere you want," I said as I watched the garbage truck turn the corner and vanish out of sight.

* * *

Anywhere she wanted ended up being the mountains of Colorado. This was an odd place to spend a romantic evening out. If you're not from Colorado you might not understand this. But most couples that live in the suburbs of the Front Range don't get a sitter and then gallivant up to the mountains for quality time. That'd be like living in D.C. and going for a night out at the White House. There are only a limited number of activities you can do in the mountains: hunt, ski, fish, hike, white water raft, and things of that sort. Other than visiting some small mountain town, there was nothing worthy of a night out in the middle of November. I couldn't imagine driving out there, Rachel giving me a fluorescent orange vest, a rifle, and then saying, "Come on, baby, we're going to go kill ourselves some deer."

But anything was possible these days.

"So where exactly are we going?" I asked Rachel.

"I've got the map right here," Rachel said clutching the printed Google map.

"But where is it?"

"It's a surprise," Rachel said.

This map didn't lead to a mountain town; it literally led into the mountains. Rachel was smiling the whole way. As we drove she tried to talk about everyday things: Lucy's grades in school, the progress of my novel, and then as we entered the mountains we delved into deeper subjects like if it was too late to have any more kids. We decided we were through having children years ago, but lately Rachel had begun to second-guess that decision. Wouldn't a baby be so adorable? Is there anything cuter than a newborn? But there were practical matters to consider. Lucy was six, so could we really just bring another kid into this family? Or should we adopt?

"Turn here," Rachel said reading the map. I obeyed and

turned off the highway. We headed down a gravel road. We didn't have an SUV and the gravel made the drive feel like a poorly put together carnival ride. It tossed us back and forth, and the farther we drove the thicker the forest grew. The trees were closing in, making me feel claustrophobic. There were lots of side roads like this in the mountains. You could turn off the main highway, drive a few miles, and civilization felt distant.

"Stop here," Rachel said. She had us stop in a tunnel. We were halfway in, equidistant from the entrance and the exit. "Turn off the car," Rachel said.

"Baby, where are we?"

"This is the seventh most haunted place in Colorado," Rachel said. *Rule #2 Only in the house* flashed through my thoughts. "I thought this would be fun." She was beaming. This was the type of look that she had on her face the first time she said *I'm pregnant* only now instead of smiling about bringing life into the world, she was proud that she'd taken me to the seventh most haunted place in Colorado on date night.

"Why are we at the seventh most haunted place in Colorado?"

"I thought we could do a little more ghost hunting."

"Rachel, we're done ghost hunting." Why did I have to tell her this? She agreed with me on the rules that we were only going to do this in the house, and even if we were going to take this out of the house there was still *Rule #5: There's an expiration date.* The research portion of my novel was through —didn't she understand that? And if she did, why were we here? "This isn't even ghost hunting, Rachel. That makes it sound like these are just friendly, wacky creatures that want to say hi to us."

"What would you call it?"

"I don't know. I don't even know why we're here."

"Because this place is special."

"Special?"

"Yes. There was a field trip out here years ago. A bus full of children was driving through this tunnel while the kids sang songs and laughed and played. They didn't even know they were in any danger until they heard the crack of a tire blowout and the bus jackknifed into the tunnel wall. Many of the children died on that bus. And now late at night if you turn your car off, small fingerprints will appear on your car and you can hear their laughter and playing—it's the echoes of what things sounded like right before they died," Rachel said.

I had no idea how to respond. She sounded like a tour guide giving a polished tour. As if she'd read up on this and had been waiting to give me this little speech. She'd probably even practiced it. Probably knew where she was going to put each inflection. "Honey, I'm just going to be honest here because I think that's what you're supposed to do in a marriage. I think you have a problem."

"A problem?"

"Yes, a problem. I mean, come on, Rachel, you're becoming obsessed with all of this. How do you even know that?"

"Well, when we were using the Ouija board in the mommy playgroup—"

"You used the Ouija board in mommy playgroup?"

"Yes, Charlie. I used to bring my favorite recipes to playgroup, but ever since I started talking about ghost hunting they wanted to know more. So, I brought the Ouija board and we had a little séance. And really it was pretty amazing. Everyone agreed that the Ouija board was so much more interesting than swapping recipes, well except one of the uptight moms who left the group and started calling the rest of us witches, but other than that we all loved having séances."

"Wait, slow down, let me get this straight. You've been having séances at mommy playgroup?"

"I didn't tell you because you've been getting all uptight about this with the rules and the—"

"Rachel, this isn't stuff you can just play around with. I've seen things—"

"I've seen things too. That's what I'm trying to tell you. Vicki heard about this place when she was a kid. So in this morning's séance we asked if it was really haunted and one of the kids from the crash visited the séance. He told us it was true. We all looked it up, and it turns out this is the seventh most haunted place in Colorado. So, I told them I'd come here and visit it and I'd give a full report. And I wanted to bring you along, Charlie, so you could see it."

"This morning?"

"Yeah."

"As in, you had a séance with mommy playgroup this morning?"

"Yes, honey."

"But I threw the Ouija board away yesterday."

"I found it in the trash. I couldn't just let you throw it away, Charlie. I wasn't done with it."

This was all my fault. I should have known better. I couldn't just introduce the supernatural to my wife and expect her to dabble with it and be satisfied. She was going to immerse herself in it like she did everything else. I couldn't let that happen. "You're done now. You're not ever using that thing again."

"Really? You're just going to make a decree like that?"

"Can you not see how you're acting? When you said take a night and get away, I thought you meant like a normal husband and wife. Not for more of this. I mean, no offense, baby, but you're starting to act a little psychotic, crazy, and obsessed."

"How am I supposed to be not offended by that?"

"I don't know."

"It sounds like you're calling me crazy."

"Well, aren't you acting just a tad bit, I mean, just a hair crazy? We're in an abandoned haunted tunnel in the middle of the mountains with our car turned off. And not just any tunnel —no!—this is the fifth most haunted place in Colorado."

"Seventh most haunted place," she corrected.

"Seventh most haunted place," I shouted. "And you know, because of the séances you've been having behind my back. And I'm supposed to take all of this like it's no big deal."

"Well, I just thought it was about time that I wasn't the only crazy one in this marriage. I know I don't need to act crazy because you've been acting plenty crazy for both of us. You quit your job, you sold our house, you moved us into a house from the 1980s with a dead lawn and preachy neighbors who bring people over to our house so they can pour oil all over everything we own. And you've also started pouring oil all over everything we own. Our house smells like the Olive Garden."

"It's cooking oil! Not olive oil."

"Whatever. You know what I mean. You're not the only one who gets to have one-liners," Rachel said.

Rule #3: Don't skimp on the Wesson Cooking Oil. How could she be complaining about that? It had kept us safe so far. And that was a problem? *Well, I'm sorry for looking out for us,* I wanted to say. But I just let her keep talking.

"You start playing with Ouija boards in the name of research and tell me you're seeing things. I think *that's* crazy. I think chairs don't just move and messages don't just appear on the bathroom mirror. But I think, I'll believe my husband. I'll have faith in him. That's when I start to see things. I even start to get fascinated with everything he's been chasing and I start to wonder if something's really out there. Only right when I'm starting to find out, my husband calls me crazy. And so I sit in a car next to him and I wonder, what sort of man am I married to?"

She grabbed my hand. It was a gesture of love and forgiveness. It was her reaching across the chasm to connect with me. But I couldn't tell if it was genuine or not. I couldn't tell if she really wanted to connect with me, or if she just wanted to placate me to go along with her plan and discover how haunted this place really was.

I told her, "You're married to a man who is trying to build a life for us. Who isn't just comfortable with the status quo. You're married to a man who was doing all of this to research his novel, not to impress the women and the tea and crumpet group!"

I pulled my hand away from hers. She responded by opening the door, getting out of the car, and slamming the door shut behind her.

I jumped out and shouted, "Rachel, come on, you can't just leave."

But she was just leaving. She was walking toward the exit of the tunnel. Not just walking. It was the quick and angry walk of a wife who was furious with her husband. She was halfway toward the exit now.

"Rachel, come back! I'm sorry. You're right. Is that what you want to hear? Okay. Great. Fine. You're married to a horrible selfish husband. You win."

My words had no effect on her. She didn't even slow down. She was almost out of the tunnel. This was really a scene out of a horror movie now. The unsuspecting wife walks into the forest where the killer is waiting. No wonder so many horror movies were set in places like this. Because there were only trees and darkness out here. If you scream, there's no one here to help you. But I was here for my wife. I wouldn't let anything happen to her. I was going to sprint after her—

And that's when I heard children playing.

I spun to see if anyone was around. There was nothing but the black arch of the tunnel. That's where the playing and laughter was coming from—the tunnel itself. I tried to make out the children's words, but they were muddy, like trying to make out the secret message in the backmasking of a heavy metal song. I strained to listen until I figured out what the children were saying:

She's ours now.

It was a song their little voices sang: *She's Ours Now.* They laughed and then repeated it again and again. I went to the car. I needed to start it and get Rachel. Why was I hanging out in the creepy haunted tunnel while Rachel was out there alone? I went to open my car and that's when I saw it.

Late at night if you turn off your car, children's fingerprints will appear—

A fingerprint appeared on the car. There was still enough moonlight so I could see it. I knelt down to look at it and that's when other tiny fingerprints appeared. As if children were walking up and pressing their hands against my car. As if their residue was left behind. I was paralyzed. I thought if there was a God, no wonder he never lets us see anything supernatural. What would we ever get done? How could we lead a normal life with these sorts of things happening all around us every day?

"Rachel!" I shouted down the tunnel. She needed to see this. But I couldn't see her. There was no angry silhouette sauntering off into the night. "Rachel!" I shouted again. No answer. I started walking toward the end of the tunnel. Where was she? I'd only been looking at that car for what, thirty seconds maybe? She couldn't have just disappeared in that time. She was just around the bend and I'd see her as soon as I got out of the tunnel.

But I didn't.

She wasn't there. I couldn't see her, I couldn't hear her, and if I'm being completely honest with you, I couldn't feel her. It felt like I was completely alone, as if there wasn't another soul around. There was only me and the darkness. "Rachel, come on. Our car's in there. I can't just leave it there. Come on out so we can go home. Are you punishing me? Is that what this is? Are you actually punishing me? Fine. I deserve to be punished. Is that what you want to hear?"

I started walking down the road. She wasn't there. I was running now. I was running as fast as I could down the gravel road that Rachel had us turn onto. With every step I pushed myself faster, thinking that I would see her. She'd be walking with her arms folded. She'd be cold and furious and she'd probably tell me, *I'm finding another ride home, Charlie.*

At least I'd see her.

That's all I wanted now. In the last five minutes I'd gone from calling my wife crazy to just wanting to see her alive. I was still running and she just wasn't there. I should have caught up to her by now, but I hadn't. I wasn't sure what to do next. Should I get my car and drive up and down the road until I found her? Should I call for help? I flipped my phone open and there was no service. I'd have to drive into town for help and that'd take at least an hour by the time I got there and back.

"Rachel!" I screamed one more time. I was crying. The fear of what could be happening to my wife was sinking in. With so many options and so many fears rushing through me, I stood on the mountain road and looked at the trees tall as skyscrapers on both sides of me, the black mouth of the tunnel smiling at me, and I wondered what exactly I should do next.

22

Young Charlie Brown

Then a thought appeared.

She's in the woods, Charlie. It was a voice in my head. It was as clear as if I'd said it out loud myself. But I hadn't been thinking that thought myself because I was so paralyzed with fear that I couldn't think straight. Still, the thought felt right. I knew it was true.

You need to go save her. You've pulled her into this and now you've got to be the one pulling her out of it.

Wait a minute. Was this my fault? Where were these words coming from? It didn't matter. I had to save her. I started walking into the woods when I heard—

Wrong way, Charlie. That's the wrong side of the forest.

"How do you know that?" I spoke these words out loud. I was really hoping I wasn't losing my mind with all of the stress of the novel and seeing paranormal events and now with Rachel disappearing. Please, don't tell me this is one of those stories with the lame twist that I was just imagining everything the whole time. If I was just imagining things, or dreaming them, then why did it even matter? Those are the worst stories there are. I scold my high school creative writing students for writing stories with that sort of twist. Certainly that's not how this book will turn out.

"I know that because I know where Rachel is," the voice said. Only this time it was clearly not in my head. It was spoken out loud. I started looking to see where the voice was coming from.

Walking out of the tunnel was someone dressed in all white.

It was Gabriel, my guardian angel. He wasn't dressed like a plumber this time; he was in all white and standing there so brightly he'd be impossible to miss. He also had a broad sword strapped to his back. Wasn't sure what he was planning to use that for. I wasn't sure about any of this. I'd seen him in a suit and dressed like a plumber, but I'd never seen him wearing white and looking so angelic like he was on that night. Apparently at the moment he didn't need to hide his true identity.

"Charlie, you've got to go into the woods and find Rachel," Gabriel said.

"What are you doing here?"

"This seemed like the type of moment where you needed your guardian angel. I'm here to help you find your wife. But you're not going to like what you see."

I didn't know what to say. How was this happening? How was my wife missing and I was standing here talking to my guardian angel and he's telling me to walk into the forest?

This all seemed like a fairy tale or a short story. Actually, it really seemed like Hawthorne.

"You're thinking of a story right now, aren't you?"

"How do you know that? Can angels read minds?"

"No. I don't think so. I'll have to ask the other guys," Gabriel said.

"Then how did you know I was thinking of a story?"

"Because, Charlie, you were raised on books and movies. You are always equating one to every situation you're in. I can't read your mind, but I know you pretty well. I am your guardian angel."

"Right."

"So what story were you thinking of?"

"*Young Goodman Brown.*"*

"Yeah, that's a good analogy."

It seemed my angel was a student of literature because he said, "You need to go find your wife just like Goodman did."

---

*As referenced earlier, *Young Goodman Brown* is one of the best American short stories ever written, about a man who's been married for three months to a woman named Faith. Yes, this name is loaded with allegorical juiciness. And no, that's not cheesy. When Hawthorne and Milton were writing, it was okay to name characters with this sort of spot-on thematic accuracy. Especially in Hawthorne's case, where the name *Faith* has double thematic meaning. She was named for her faithfulness to Goodman and because she encapsulated his faith in God. In this story Goodman Brown is coaxed into the woods by a seemingly supernatural creature. (It was actually Satan/ the devil in Hawthorne's version, not a guardian angel, but still.) Goodman complied and began his journey, which climaxed with the young husband finding not only his wife, but all of the people of Salem—friends, mentors, and everyone else he knew—knee-deep in debauchery and rolling around in witchcraft. Goodman Brown lost his faith (again, both his wife's faithfulness and faith in God). It changed Young Goodman Brown's outlook not only on his wife, but also on all of the friends and his entire community for the rest of his life before he died a bitter old man.

Was my angel saying I was supposed to make some super-natural quest into the woods? And what would I find there? Or lose? No time to think about all of that. I needed to find Rachel and I'd do whatever it took.

"Are you ready?" Gabriel asked.

"Yes, I'm very ready."

"Okay, great, but you should probably move your car first," Gabriel said. "I'd hate to see what would happen if another car went speeding in there when their guardian angel wasn't working."

* * *

We made our way through the forest. The terrain was unstable because we weren't following a trail. There were rocks, branches, dead leaves, pinecones, and who knows what other sort of dead forest debris crunching under our feet as we went toward Rachel. We went slowly because I couldn't see much in the dark. I'm not sure if I would have been able to see at all if my angel's obnoxiously white outfit didn't help light up our trail.

We didn't talk at first; just one step after another in an awkward silence. But as I looked at my angel with his long flowing hair and crystal blue eyes and the Middle Earth sword strapped to his back, I thought, how often do people get a chance to walk by their guardian angel? Shouldn't I maximize this? I have so many questions about faith and religion; shouldn't I ask this guy right here when there's nothing else to talk about anyway? Besides, maybe if I asked questions it would take my mind off of imagining the worst things that could be happening to Rachel right now. We'd walk into a clearing and she'd be stabbed to death. I'd grab her and hold her dead, limp, lifeless body in my arms as I screamed—

Stop.

I looked at my guardian angel and asked, "Are you around all the time?"

"Around what?"

"Around me."

"Some of the time," Gabriel said.

"Are you around when I go to sleep or go to the bathroom?"

"I'm your guardian angel. Not your stalker."

"Then when are you around?"

"When you need protection."

"How do you know when I need protection?"

"I just have a sense about these things."

"Are you good at your job?"

"Very good at my job."

"Are most guardian angels good at their jobs?" I said.

"Yes, we're all really talented at what we do. They don't just make anyone a guardian angel."

"It's just … nothing. We need to focus on finding Rachel."

"No, come on, say it."

"It's just there are still deaths every day. Car wrecks, homicides, accidents, fires, floods, earthquakes, robberies, car jackings, domestic violence, electrocutions, radiation poisoning, and I don't know what else—those are just a few things off the top of my head. I mean, I think there's a stat, like someone dies of unnatural causes every second in America alone. I'm not sure what the exact stat is, but I'm sure it's something like that. A lot of deaths all the time. So, you know, I hear you bragging that all of you guys are doing a good job, but to me, as an outsider, it looks like the guardian angels of the world are dropping the ball quite a bit."

"Wow, I've never thought of it like that. That's a really good point," Gabriel said. I could hear the sarcasm in his voice. Do I just bring the sarcastic side out of everyone?

"You've never thought of it like that?" I said in a deadpan tone.

"Actually, oh wait, I have. Let me tell you something, Charlie: if we weren't around, most people wouldn't live past the age of five. Do things still happen? Sure, of course things still happen. Lots of reasons for that. Maybe it's just their time, or maybe it's that 2 to 3 percent of the time where someone just couldn't be saved. That's still 97 percent of the time when we're saving your lives. You all are crazy. The way you drive with your cell phones and the way you eat and the way you attack each other. Human beings can make a weapon out of absolutely anything. It's really disturbing for us angels if you want me to be quite honest. The truth is, every guardian angel I know is working overtime. So, yes, people still die in America and there are deaths all over the world. Every day. But do you know who doesn't die almost every day? Most people. Most people are just fine. And if it weren't for us they would be a lot less fine. We're pulling so many people out of the fires I wish you could see it. Honestly, this is all really complicated. Even I don't understand how it all works. What I do know, is that by my count, you should have died around 34 times by now. And I've saved you every one of those times. And you know, we may even come to 35 or 36 tonight. So please, you can ask questions, but at least show a little gratitude. At least don't act like you know exactly how everything works. You're better than that. At least I really hope you're better than that; otherwise I've been working overtime to save a complete jerk."

I couldn't believe my angel just called me a jerk. I actually didn't know how to respond to anything he said. Here I was thinking I was so clever with all of my questions, but what I didn't anticipate is my angel must have been asked stuff like this all the time.

"I'm a good guy," I said.

"Well, okay," Gabriel replied, "start acting like one."

"I was just asking questions."

"Questions are fine."

"Did God send you?"

"Yes."

"Is God going to let something happen to my wife?"

"God doesn't just let something happen —"

Gabriel didn't finish his speech. Because that's when we saw Rachel crouched under a tree and shivering. We walked over a hill, and at the bottom of it Rachel was sitting there underneath a mammoth pine tree. She had her jacket on and her pearl necklace; she looked like the same beautiful woman I married thirteen years ago.

Except thirteen years ago there weren't creatures crawling all around her.

"What are those?"

"They're demons, Charlie."

There were four demons — creatures without clothes; their skin was a light grey, but I could see veins and bruises all over their bodies. They looked just like the things crawling all over Lucy during spaghetti dinner night. They slithered around my wife snarling; their eyes glowed a bright yellow like a cat fresh out of the grave.

"Rachel!" I shouted.

She snapped her head up and looked at me. Her eyes told me that she was furious with me; that she hadn't forgiven me for the fight in the car. But who cared about that? Could she not see those creatures crawling all around her? Surely, she couldn't. There is no way she would just sit there that calmly if she saw those grey-skinned beasts snarling at her.

"Rachel, I'm sorry. What are you doing down there?"

My wife continued to just glare at me.

"Honey, you're going to freeze to death. Come on, we have to go."

"I'm not going anywhere with you. Ever again," Rachel snarled. The creatures kept crawling back and forth and she didn't notice. They were sniffing. Licking. Curling around her. Why couldn't she feel it? Why was I the only one to see what was going on there?

"What's wrong with her?" I said.

"The demons sense an opportunity," Gabriel said.

"What do you mean they sense an opportunity?"

"She's inviting darkness in. She's been chasing this stuff, Charlie. You both have and the creatures can smell it: the Ouija board, Bloody Mary, the pictures, telling her group all about everything she's seen — she doesn't just have a mild interest in all of this. She's passionate about it. That's all these demons live for, Charlie. They're as dumb as doorposts, but they're always hungry. They see when they have a victim and they're like mosquitoes to blood. When they see an opportunity, they suck the marrow out of it."

"Why can she not see what's going on?"

"Because I've given you a gift, Charlie. Tonight I wanted you to see what's really happening with your wife. Tomorrow you won't be able to see any of this. But I keep telling you to be careful with all of this, to change your ways, and Charlie, honestly you're one of the most stubborn clients I have. You just won't listen. So, I thought if I can't tell you what's going on, maybe I can show it to you."

I thought about what my angel said. It made sense. Not that it mattered right now. I couldn't think about what all of this meant. What I knew was my wife was out in the middle of the forest freezing with demons all around her and I needed to put an end to this. I started walking down to her and the creatures looked up at me. They were like Rottweilers when you get near a piece of meat they're chewing on.

One creature looked right at me.

It charged.

It was on all fours running at me. It lunged in the air. I froze. I didn't have the quickness to be able to move or run or duck. I wish I could tell you that I did some sort of ninja roll to get out of the way of the creature. But I was much too frightened for that—I was too terrified to do anything but stand like a deer in headlights and watch the oncoming semitruck of a demon charge at me. It reached toward me and opened its fangs; its hands were on my shoulders right up to the point that a broad sword swung right in front of me and cut the creature in half.

The two pieces of it fell in front of me.

The other creatures looked up. They were just as crazy and they started running toward me. But Gabriel was standing in front of me now. One creature lunged, but before it could get anywhere near me Gabriel thrust the sword right into its gut. It squealed and its insides sprayed everywhere like a watermelon hit with a sledgehammer. Another creature ran at me; this time Gabriel swung the sword down on top of it. Its head rolled on the ground.

The final creature was standing near Rachel.

It could see the fate of its friends. So it didn't charge at me or my sword-wielding guardian angel. Instead it ran at Rachel and jumped inside of her. I'm not sure how exactly, it just jumped toward Rachel and disappeared inside of her. Rachel physically reacted when it happened. Her whole body twitched for a moment like she could feel the darkness inside of her. Then there was silence. No more creatures snarling or dying.

"Rachel," I said. But she didn't make a sound. It looked like she was in a trance. "What happened?" I asked Gabriel.

"Come on," Gabriel said. "We've got to get her out of here before more of them come."

23

Demonic Roadkill

I had to carry Rachel all the way back to the car. I asked my angel if there was any way he could help and he said no. I said, "You can decapitate demons but you can't help me carry my wife?" And he said, "Pretty much." So it was just me carrying Rachel—half in a trance and half passed out—back to the car. There were no other creatures that appeared as we walked through the forest, but I could feel them smiling and snarling at us. Gabriel had his sword out and looked around, making any demon think twice about attacking. My arms were stretched and thin so I had to carry her on my hip for the last half mile to the car. But we did get back, and it was parked right where I left it outside the tunnel.

I tried to sit Rachel in the passenger seat, but she was completely passed out and wouldn't sit up. She slumped over the armrest and cup holders. I was sure such an uncomfortable position would wake her up. It didn't. She lay there—

(What is wrong with her? She shouldn't be this out of it. Is she in a coma or did that creature do something to her?)

— passed out. I couldn't tell what was going on with her. Part of me wanted to wake her up and talk with her. The other part of me thought if she did wake up she'd probably snarl, bite my neck, and try to strangle me the way the other demons did.

I picked her back up — I didn't even know if I could lift her again, my arms were so weak — and placed her in the backseat. Her body was Silly Putty, able to move and shift in any position. I shut the door and walked around the car. I stopped in front of the tunnel. I thought about the handprints appearing, the whispers, and I wondered if I walked down that black corridor right now how many of those creatures I would see. What would they do to me if I walked in there? No time for that. Gabriel was standing next to me with his sword still drawn and he seemed to agree.

"We should go, Charlie."

I got in the car and Gabriel hopped in the passenger seat. It wasn't even weird to me at this point that my angel was riding shotgun with me. I flicked on my headlights, and that's when I saw several (five or maybe as many as seven) creatures crawling in front of the car. These weren't deer or raccoons or possums or any other forest creatures. These were creatures of darkness just like the ones that were around Rachel: grey skin, yellow eyes, and snarling. How many more of them were coming?

"Drive, Charlie," Gabriel said.

I was paralyzed just like before. Maybe there's a better word. I was more mesmerized at being able to look at these creatures for the first time without distraction. They seemed so thirsty for something, they seemed—

"Drive!" Gabriel screamed.

I slammed my foot on the gas. My tires spun, my car leapt forward, and all of the demons scattered like pigeons. Why did they scatter like that? Can a car hit demons? Is there such a thing as demonic roadkill? The car sped down the mountain road, jumping up and down on the rocks and the gravel as I went. I glanced into the forest, and it seemed like there were yellow eyes peeking through the trees everywhere. But I wasn't going to slow down. I needed to push this sedan as fast as I could.

Finally, I took a right and pulled onto the mountain highway and away from the seventh most haunted place in Colorado. Nothing felt better than smooth asphalt. My soul was already getting calmer just by having felt like I'd escaped something, something I wasn't supposed to see. I was shaking, still unable to lift my foot up from mashing the car pedal against the floor, as my car sped down the mountain highway.

"What was that?"

"You're going really fast. I don't want to have to jump out of this car and save you from getting into a wreck," Gabriel said. "Slow down and I'll answer any of your questions."

It took strength and focus but I lifted my foot off the gas pedal. "Thank you," Gabriel said. "Now what exactly do you want to know about?"

"What is happening to my wife? Why did one of them jump into my wife?"

"So it could possess her."

"So it could ..."

"Possess her," Gabriel said again.

"You're telling me my wife is demon possessed?" I still had my hand clutched tightly to the steering wheel, and I watched the oncoming headlights pass by me as I drove down the mountain road. I wouldn't be surprised at this point if I looked over and saw a demon driving one of the cars that was passing by.

"I know this is crazy, Charlie. That's why we don't let most people see everything that you've been seeing. It's kind of the last resort. Even when we do let people see the truth they assume A) they're dreaming or B) they're hallucinating/crazy."

"I don't really care. All I want to know is how to get my wife back to normal."

"That's the most thoughtful thing I've heard you say all night."

"Good. So what can I do to save her?"

"There's nothing you can do."

"There has to be something."

"There's not. God is the only one who can save her now."

* * *

The sitter was asleep on the couch. I walked in holding my wife like a groom holding his bride. Only my wife was dead asleep and our clothes were tattered and they smelled like the forest. I kicked the door open and the sitter sat up, peeked over the couch, and rubbed the sleep out of her eyes. She stared at me with this dazed expression, her face asking *Am I dreaming this?* I couldn't blame her. I'd been thinking the same thing all night.

"How were the kids?" I asked.

"Um, they were fine ..." she said. She couldn't stop staring at Rachel.

"Oh, she's not dead," I told the sitter.

"Um, great. That's good," the sitter said.

I laid Rachel down on the couch and took out my wallet. "Here's for the kids and here's an extra fifty dollars. Sorry we were so late."

"Thank you," she said. She grabbed her stuff and left my house as quickly as she possibly could. Who knows what she was thinking? Not that it really mattered at the moment. I didn't have time or energy to worry about the sitter just then.

I ran to the kitchen and opened the pantry. *Rule #3: Don't skimp on the Wesson Cooking Oil.* I grabbed the large bottle out and I was a little surprised to see it was almost empty. How was it almost empty? I only used a little bit every time. Was this actually a barometer of how knee-deep in supernatural activity we had been? I would have asked Gabriel, but he wouldn't even come inside with me. When I parked the car he said, "The rest is up to you. Good luck, Charlie." I wasn't sure how to say goodbye to my angel. I wasn't even sure what to feel about him. He'd helped me, but he wasn't doing much now when I needed him the most. So I just said, "See you around, Gabriel."

I tucked the bottle of oil under my arm, picked up Rachel, and we went upstairs. Once she was on the bed I dabbed a bit of oil on my fingers and then smeared it on her forehead. I prayed: *Please, let her be okay. Please, let whatever that thing is inside of her leave her alone. Just turn my wife back to normal. Okay? We're through. I swear we're through. We'll never do any of this again. I've learned my lesson once and for all. I'm sorry I didn't learn it sooner. I'm a slow learner; I'm nearly dyslexic when it comes to spiritual things. Just please let my wife be okay.*

It felt like my prayers were working, like something was really happening inside of her. I didn't see her eyes turn yellow; she didn't foam at the mouth and scream in a guttural voice; she didn't do any of the stuff that seemed common in exorcisms. But maybe that was just the stuff of movies. Maybe she'd been healed and it was more like when someone was cured of cancer and suddenly they were just okay again and they start rebuilding their life. But just in case, I planned to stay awake until she woke up. I didn't want Adam and Lucy to have to deal with a demon-possessed mother.

I'd stay awake until she woke up the next morning.

I would not fall asleep.

I would not—

24

Wake Up, Sleepyhead

I had my clothes on from the night before when I woke up. The same slacks, the same button-up shirt, and I still smelled like I'd been camping for the last week. I tried to orient myself; the last thing I remembered was putting oil on Rachel's forehead—

Rachel.

She was leaning over me.

I woke up and she was leaning over me. Her face was inches away from mine. Her breath was warm. My eyes snapped open. I remembered last night—the demons, the creatures, the yellow eyes, and the snarling. Was that Rachel right now? Was she about to do something to me?

I winced waiting for the worst.

She kissed me on the cheek. "Wake up, sleepyhead."

I sat up in my bed. It was morning now—sweet morning with its fresh scent and chirping birds and promise of a great day. Rachel sure didn't seem demon possessed. She seemed like a happy, well-adjusted housewife. She had a new outfit, an apron, and the perfect amount of makeup on. She looked like she'd just walked off the cover of a 1960s cookbook. "You must be really tired after everything that happened last night," Rachel said as she folded some clothes and put them away. "Wake up. Breakfast is ready."

Rachel left the room. I changed my clothes and then followed her. What was I following her to? Was she still demon possessed? Would there be pentagrams drawn all over the fridge in goat's blood?

There was nothing like that.

When I got downstairs it was a morning just like any other. Adam and Lucy were eating bacon and eggs while Rachel was scrubbing the pans clean. I walked into the kitchen and my kids said hello to me and then went back to their breakfasts. "I left a plate of bacon and eggs for you on the table," Rachel said.

I sat down and began to eat my breakfast, but the whole time I was staring at my family. How were things this normal after last night? Rachel had said, You must be really tired after everything that happened last night. But what exactly did she remember? Did she remember the fight, and being so upset that she ran deep into the forest and was out there alone for over an hour? Did she remember that when I finally found her, I was with my guardian angel, who was dressed in white and holding a broad sword, the same sword he used to decapitate a couple of demons before one finally jumped inside her? Because if she did remember those things, how was she just making breakfast like this was just another Sunday morning?

Adam and Lucy finished eating and took their plates to

Rachel. She told them, "You can watch TV, but only for a half hour and then you need to clean your rooms."

"Okay, Mom," they both said right before they scampered off. Rachel was beaming as she watched them leave. Then she looked at me with this June Cleaver look that said, Kids— you've got to love 'em. I still couldn't believe it. My whole life I've been a man plagued by doubt, and on that morning I doubted that she wasn't being influenced by the supernatural. I stood behind her still waiting for the other shoe to drop. Was she about to turn into her full-fledged demonic self? Would she start screaming at me and flying around the room once the kids were out of eyesight?

Or did the Wesson Oil once again work its miracles?

The last thing I remembered was sitting over her dabbing oil on her head and praying for everything to go back to normal. Well, maybe my prayer had been answered. But I needed to find out for sure. I needed to ask her something to see if she really was her "normal" self.

"Rachel," I said.

"Yes, honey," she answered.

"We need to talk about last night."

"Okay," she answered. "But first let me say something."

"Sure."

"I'm sorry," she said.

There was a lot to be sorry for, but I wasn't sure what exactly she was referring to. "Sorry for ..."

"The way things went. Yes, I thought I'd spring something on you. Thought I'd take us to a place to see something; I'd been thinking about it for a while, but how were you supposed to know that? What a shock it must have been that I took us to that place. No wonder you reacted like you did. But last night I was just frustrated you didn't see things *my* way so I stormed off. It was so dangerous. Then you went out there to find me and save me. And that's why I want to be as kind as I can this morning. I want to show you how sorry I really am."

I wanted to believe her apology was sincere—but it sounded hollow and distant, like the way Greg and Marcia talk at the end of a *Brady Bunch* episode. Still, she didn't sound demon possessed, unless people who are demon possessed sound like the Bradys, which I guess is entirely possible.

"Is that all you remember?"

"For the most part."

"You don't remember seeing anything?"

"No, I left before I could even see the fingerprints on the car. Did it work? Could you see the fingerprints?"

"Yeah, among other things."

"What other things?"

"I saw creatures. And they weren't ghosts or goblins or apparitions—they were demons, Rachel. They were crawling all over you. They were sniffing you, they were—"

"Wait, they were what?" My wife looked at her hands, her arms, she looked like she felt dirty by the way I was talking about her.

"I know. I couldn't believe it either. That's why I wanted to know if you saw something."

"I didn't see anything. All I was thinking was I wanted to get away from you. I thought I really wanted to show you how angry I was. I was going to walk back to the highway and hitchhike into town. Only I didn't want to walk down the gravel road; I thought I could cut across and get there quicker."

"Then what do you remember?"

"I don't know exactly. I remember pretty soon I couldn't see where I was going. I tried to get out my cell phone to call you, but there was no service. I got so cold I couldn't walk anymore. So I just sat under that tree. I don't even really know what my plan was at that point. It felt like I was in a trance."

"Well, that's where I found you. And you looked like you were in a trance, but there were also creatures—

(Or is she telling the real version? Is she telling the truth and you were the one imagining things? Gabriel didn't lift her up. Gabriel didn't do anything but cut a demon in half and maybe that was just something you imagined.)

—crawling all over and you didn't even seem to notice," I said.

"I didn't see anything. All I know is I was angry with you, angry about being there; I was blaming you for everything. If you say there were creatures, then I believe you because I felt the darkness last night. At one point I was under that tree and I thought I might die out there."

Tears were streaming down her face. I put my arms around her and held her, soaking in the warmth between us. I kissed her on the crown of her head and said, "It's over now and everything's going to be okay. We're moving out of here as soon as we can. I've had enough of this."

* * *

That night we prepared a meal of chicken fried steak and country potatoes. Lucy and I were setting the table while

Adam filled everyone's glasses with ice. We were the all-American family prepping for dinner when there was a knock at the door.

"I'll get it," Adam said.

"Keep getting everyone's drinks," I said. "I'll get the door." It was probably just someone selling Girl Scout cookies or magazine subscriptions. I would open the door and tell them it was dinnertime and we weren't interested.

It wasn't the Girl Scouts.

I peeked out the window and saw two large white vans parked in our driveway. The rear doors were open on both of them and men hauled large pieces of equipment out of the back of the vans. These looked like the type of guys who would hang out at comic book conventions, but they weren't at a comic book convention; they were at my house and they had computers and cameras scattered all over my driveway and lawn.

As I opened the door, they were in mid conversation. "Where should I put the EMF reader? Can I just fasten it—"

When they realized the door was open, the conversation stopped. We all just stood there for a moment. Finally I said, "Hello."

"Hello. Are you Mr. Walker?" the guy standing closest to the door said. He seemed to be the ringleader. He was an African American with a goatee and glasses. His voice had this direct and confident tone, as if he were the good cop of this group.

"Yes, I'm Mr. Walker," I said.

"Great. My partner here wants to know where he can attach the EMF reader."

"What's an EMF reader?"

"It detects electromagnetic fields."

"Hey Dante," one of the other workers yelled. "How many cameras do you think I'll need?"

"Probably five for a house this size," Dante decided.

"Wait, slow down," I said.

"Sorry to move so fast. It's just, we've got to get everything set up if we're going to catch anything. We only have one night."

"Catch what?" I knew what they were here for. I knew why they were here. I even knew who called them. Still, I played the part of the confused man of the house. "What are you trying to catch? Why would you want to detect electromagnetic fields?"*

"That's one of the key signs of a haunting."

"Who are you?" I was asking a question I already knew the answer to.

"We're the ghost hunters your wife called," Dante said. "She told us you'd had some hauntings at your home. Isn't that true? Are we at the right house?"

* * *

Within ten minutes there were wires, cables, computers, monitors, cameras, and microphones on sticks. The gadgets in my house made my ghost hunting equipment look bush

---

*Come to find out, many in the ghost hunting community use the EMF readers to detect the supernatural. The Ghost Hunters of Syfy channel fame made this gadget popular, but many others have been using it for years. The thinking is that ghosts emit electromagnetic energy, so spiked readings may indicate spirits and ghosts in a location.

league. I was the junior detective trying to play along with the big boys. These guys were the pros. They were focused and yelling at one another as they threw spools of cable back and forth and mounted cameras on my wall. It didn't take them long at all to make our rental home look like a large ghost hunting laboratory.

"Could you show me where your circuit breaker is?" Dante asked. I looked over at Rachel eating chicken fried steak with the kids. I looked at her to say *What is going on here?* but she furrowed her eyebrows in a way that said *Just show them the box.*

I hadn't even invited these guys in. I just stood at the door not sure what to do with Dante and the men in the white van. Dante handed me his card. The front said "Dante Webber *Ghosts Inc.*" And the back said:

"Think Your House Is Haunted?

We'll find the proof you're looking for."

Before I could even send these guys away, Rachel walked right past me and said, "Come on in. We're so glad you're here." That was all the men needed to hear. Quickly a parade of them came with enough equipment to hunt for ghosts in a skyscraper. I looked at Rachel to stop it, but with her mouth she formed the word *Please.* Now I was taking Dante down to the basement to show him where my circuit breaker was. I wanted to see how good Dante was, so I asked, "Can you feel anything supernatural down here?"

"Can I *feel* anything?"

"This is where a lot of the activity has taken place. So I thought you might be able to sense something."

"I'm not in the business of sensing anything, Mr. Walker.

I'm in the business of finding proof. If your home is haunted, we'll find visual, audio, or electromagnetic evidence. Feelings aren't much evidence, are they, Mr. Walker?"

"I guess not," I said. "Here," I added, opening the circuit breaker. Dante started fidgeting around inside. I asked him, "Have you found many haunted houses?"

"No," he said.

"How many?"

"Seven confirmed. Three probable."

"That's it?"

"That's it," he said.

"How long have you been doing this?"

"Over six years." He slammed the circuit breaker shut.

Dante went upstairs and told his men what he'd learned from the circuit breaker. I sat at the table with my family. My chicken fried steak was cold and my gravy had turned to Jell-O. Adam said, "Dad, Mom said these were scientists. Do you think they'll find any ghosts?"

"You told him they were looking for ghosts?"

"What should I tell him?" Rachel asked.

"You shouldn't have to tell him anything. He shouldn't be around this."

"I'm not scared, Dad. I want to see a ghost," my son said. "Have you ever seen a ghost?"

Well, I saw one jump into your mother last night. Except they're not called "ghosts," son. They're called demons. And they're much worse than ghosts because they can control us like a puppet on strings.

This would be the honest answer if I could have been honest with my son. Of course I couldn't tell Adam that; honestly

I didn't know what I should tell him. What does a responsible parent tell their child about the paranormal?

I looked at Rachel. "Can I talk to you for a minute?" We walked outside where the men continued to load equipment out of the vans and into our house. "How much stuff do they have?"

"I don't know," Rachel said.

"You're the one who called them," I said.

"I called them because they were the best ghost hunting agency in Colorado. Charlie, they don't just take cases. Normally, it takes months for them to even come at all. But when I sent them the pictures we took and wav files of the noises we heard, they seemed really interested."

"And you didn't tell me they were coming?"

"I didn't think they would," she said.

"They shouldn't be here, Rachel. Not in the middle of dinner and not around Adam and Lucy. My eight-year-old son is asking me if I believe in ghosts."

"Well, do you believe in ghosts?"

"I believe in demons."

"I thought you said they were the same thing," my wife said.

"Well, I didn't know what I was talking about then. Now I know ghosts turn the faucet on and off in the middle of the night. They flicker the lights and make it a little colder in the fridge. Demons are creatures that torment and destroy."

"You're saying the difference between ghosts and demons is ghosts mess with appliances?"

"I didn't say I was an expert on all of this. But I have seen things. And I sure saw something last night. I can't call what

I saw "ghosts" because that makes them sound friendly and cute — maybe a little mischievous and creepy. But a demon is different. You said it yourself. You said they sounded gross. Well, they are gross — I told you what they were doing to you and one of them jumped *inside* you, Rachel. And I think it would have jumped inside me if Gabriel hadn't sliced it in half. Does that sound crazy? Yes. Is it what I saw? Yes, it is."

"That's the thing, Charlie. I didn't *see* anything. I had something spelled out to me by some kid who died in the bus crash. I wanted to prove that I really heard something through the Ouija board by seeing the fingerprints. But you attacked me as soon as we got there. I wandered off into the forest where apparently you saw demons and angels battle like they were in Greek mythology — I saw nothing. Not one thing, Charlie. I still can't make sense of all of this. And I don't really want to just pack up and leave before I understand what happened here. It'd be like walking out in the middle of a scary movie."

I knew what Rachel was doing. When we were dating, a movie revival house near our campus was showing *Seven*. Neither of us had seen it, and I wanted to see it because it was a horror and she wanted to see it because it had Brad Pitt. But she walked out in the middle of the movie. She couldn't handle seeing people killed by their own lust, gluttony, and greed. She couldn't stand to watch John Doe torture anyone else with their own vices. As she stood up she looked at me, but I said I wanted to stay. I ate popcorn and watched *Seven* all the way until its shocking conclusion. Rachel didn't break up with me after that and I knew it was another reason we'd get married. Still, in the lobby she told me, "I can't believe you stayed through that. That was horrible."

I told her, "My imagination is so much worse. If I don't watch a movie like that all the way until the end, I play out all the different scenarios. I keep thinking about what would have happened. I'd rather just let the movie resolve and move on."

I understood needing things to resolve. That's what my wife was asking for. Yes, it could still be a little scary, but then it would be over. And honestly, I didn't know if what was in our house were ghosts or demons, but if these guys were as good as Rachel said they were, they should be able to find something. "Listen, Rachel, I love you. I want to put all of this behind us. So I can agree to let them come in here and search for whatever they need to search for. But once we have proof that something is here, you have to promise me that we'll put all of this behind us."

"Yes, of course, Charlie. I can promise that. I just want to know what's really here," Rachel said. She hugged me and I held her for a moment. She was so warm, and there was so much love radiating between us, that for a moment I almost forgot we were surrounded by a group of men with unkempt facial hair who were about to tear our home apart looking for demons.

25

Nothing but the Proof

We checked into the Castle Rock Holiday Inn around midnight. It felt strange. We were tourists in our own town. Rachel held Lucy like a sack of overweight groceries while Adam explored the lobby. He was an insomniac loaded full of adrenaline. He couldn't get enough of the computers and night vision cameras aimed around our house. He kept pointing at the monitors and saying, "Dad, I think that's a ghost!" Rachel was just as excited. She'd look at the screens and say, "Is that an Orb?" Or she'd notice, "The EMF readings look a little high over in that corner." I couldn't believe how knowledgeable she was. I shouldn't have been surprised—again a new interest got a hold of Rachel and swallowed her whole. She didn't want to just let these guys hunt for ghosts; she wanted to be involved in the process. And it was about the fifth time she said, "Look, there's an apparition in the basement!" that Dante told us, "Maybe you should find a place to stay tonight."

* * *

"One night? Is that all you'll need?"

"Yes," I replied and handed the middle-aged woman with dirty blonde hair my credit card. She didn't even look at me. I wondered what she'd done with her life that she ended up at the midnight shift at the Holiday Inn. Maybe she'd had a good career at one point. Maybe in a month or so that would be me, standing right next to her checking in travelers and adulterers at all hours of the night because I'd failed at writing a worthwhile book. I didn't believe in hell yet, but I believed in a purgatory, and perhaps purgatory was the graveyard shift at the Holiday Inn.

Rachel put Lucy on the cot and I flopped our overnight bag onto the floor. I told Adam, "Get ready for bed" and went into the bathroom. I looked at the bars of soap wrapped in paper, tiny shampoo bottles, and folded white towels. My own bathroom was just a mile down the road. At least here there wouldn't be any messages written on the mirror.

(Or will the demons follow you wherever you go? They were deep in the mountains of Colorado. Surely, they could be in a Holiday Inn.)

I watched my reflection as I brushed my teeth. I was looking worse. Paler, older, weaker, greyer — seemed like these last few months had taken a few years out of me. Maybe that's also why I wanted to write a book. It was immortality. It was a time capsule, a piece of me that would never change no matter how much my body deteriorated.

I flicked the light off in the bathroom. Adam was already

lying on his sleeping bag; the adrenaline wore off like a bad sugar high and now he'd crashed.

Rachel was fidgety. She messed with the bedspread and put all of Adam's clothes in the suitcase. She refolded our overnight bag worth of clothing about six times. When the bag couldn't get any more organized she clicked on the TV. I knew for Rachel—and who am I kidding, for me too—our thoughts were with our home. What were they doing there? What were they finding? What proof would they have for us? Were they finally going to give us the answers we were looking for—answers that would help make sense of all the ups and downs and fear and excitement and torment we'd been experiencing for the last couple of months?

We'd have to wait until morning.

We thought we'd fall asleep. But we didn't. We sat there all night staring at the TV, listening to the talk shows and infomercials, and waiting to hear the verdict on just how haunted our home really was.

* * *

When the sun finally rose, the morning didn't feel full of promise. Rachel and I just felt exhausted. Adam and Lucy didn't look much better. Our eyes were bloodshot and everything looked overexposed and annoyingly bright. All four of us walked through the hotel lobby looking as comfortable as vampires in daylight while the other guests looked so refreshed. We drove down the street and saw people walking their dogs and jogging and we were annoyed at them for seeming so perky. We crawled into Starbucks where everyone was getting made-to-order lattes in order to embark on a bright and productive day. Rachel and I felt like we didn't have any productivity left in us. We just wanted to get the report about our home. We wanted to hear the ghost hunters say, "This is the most haunted house we've ever seen." Those words would validate everything. They'd let Rachel know we weren't crazy; they'd let me know we could move on.

Then we could sleep.

The ghost hunters were wrapping up by the time we arrived. They packed away cameras, loaded monitors into large black cases, and wound up cords. Dante was in the middle of it all directing traffic. When he saw Rachel and I walk in the house he smiled. He was a man with good news that he couldn't wait to deliver.

I told Adam and Lucy, "Go up to your rooms and unpack."

"But Dad, I want to hear about the ghosts."

"I'll tell you later. Go," I said. Adam kicked the dirt and sulked upstairs. He was his mother's son. He didn't want to play video games or freeze tag; he wanted to be around the paranormal. He'd always been like that; the things kids do don't interest him—he'd rather be with the adults. He was eight going on thirty-five.

"Good morning, Mr. and Mrs. Walker," Dante said, practically singing our names. His grin lit up his face as he handed us a three-ringed binder. I grabbed it and flipped through it: graphs, charts, numbers, and other data that I couldn't quite understand. "Here are all of our findings," Dante said.

"Um, okay, thank you," I said.

"What is this? What does all of this mean?" Rachel asked.

"In here are the pictures our camera took, thermal readings throughout the night, charts of the EMF activity in your home, and graphs with any other activity we charted."

"So how haunted is our house?" Rachel asked.

"That's just the thing, Mrs. Walker, your house isn't haunted at all. That's the good news I have for you."

Rachel and I looked at each other in disbelief. He was joking. He seemed like a man who always went straight to the facts, but surely the facts were wrong in this instance. "What?" Rachel asked. "What are you telling us? How is this good news?"

"Most people are happy to hear their house isn't haunted. It means they don't have to move. It means their lives can go back to normal."

"I don't care about this house!" Rachel shouted. "All I want to know is that we really saw something in there. And we *have* seen a lot, so I don't understand how you didn't see anything."

"I'm sorry, Mrs. Walker. We just don't have any proof of any paranormal activity whatsoever," Dante said.

"What about the things that I sent to get you here? The recordings, the pictures ..."

"There was no evidence to back that up."

"No evidence?" Rachel screamed.

"Your electromagnetic readings were really low. This picture, yes it looks like something could be happening, but there's a mirror in the background. Pictures with mirrors are always thrown out in paranormal circles. The reflection of the photographer combined with the flash can produce some freaky images. But that's not proof. You bought the cheapest digital voice recorder on the market. Those things are infamous for having distorted sounds. And so sure, it sounds like something could be happening, but it's probably just some distortion in the recording. We'll analyze it a little further, but I doubt we'll find anything. You've told stories of hauntings happening in the bathrooms, in that wood-paneled wall of yours, but all of our recordings were ice cold for any sort of paranormal readings. To be completely honest, Mrs. Walker, last night was a waste of time for us. Your house is as free from any signs of ghosts or hauntings as any we've seen in the last few months. But that's okay, because for the most part, our job is to prove houses aren't haunted. And we can say there is nothing out of the ordinary going on in your home."

Rachel stumbled back. It looked like she'd been shot. She wanted to scream or cry or shout, but she couldn't do any of that. This ghost hunter just pried apart her ribcage and pulled out her heart. She needed validation and this man spit in her face. But to me standing there, surrounded by the ghost hunters who were telling me there were no ghosts in my home, I had an epiphany.

Proof is fool's gold.

Is there any way to really prove what had happened? If we'd gotten a bunch of charts that showed dramatic drops in temperature, would that really have made me feel better? If I'd been given a graph that said there were ghosts or demons in my home, would that have really mattered? I don't think so. Not anymore. If someone believes that none of this (and by *this* I mean angels, demons, the supernatural, and so on …) exists I can completely understand it. I was right there with them for most of my life. But that's before I'd experienced the voice, the images, the feelings. That was before I was on a first-name basis with my guardian angel and I'd almost ran over demons with my car.

Are those experiences crazy?

Yes, they are.

But I'm not the only person who's experienced something — since people have been communicating, they have been telling stories about ghosts and apparitions and things that go bump in the night. Are those beliefs just our own fears? Maybe for you, you can chalk it up to my mind playing tricks on me. But I've seen enough to at least be open to the possibility that there's a lot more out there than meets the naked eye (or the naked EMF reader). How can we prove that? We can't. Can we? If we could disprove God, all religion would go away. If we could prove the supernatural, everyone would believe in ghosts, God, Satan, and guardian angels. Neither of those things can be proven. The debate rages on. There will always be people who like to prove the supernatural; and there will always be people looking to disprove God (or Satan). I needed to stop asking the questions that I began this book with: *Does God exist? Does Satan exist?* The only question I really needed to ask was *What am I going to put my faith in?*

Rachel, however, did not have the same epiphany.

Her eyes glowed yellow. She screamed at Dante, "I didn't ask you if there was electromagnetic activity in my house! I don't care about that!"

"Mrs. Walker, EMF activity is one of the key ways to detect ghosts and apparitions. Everyone in the paranormal community is in agreement about that."

"You want to see ghosts? I will show you ghosts." Rachel grabbed Dante's hand and dragged him inside. "Enough games!" Rachel shouted.

Dante looked frightened. And if he wasn't frightened, at the very least he was rattled; pretty amazing considering this guy hunted ghosts professionally. You would assume not much would rattle him. But Rachel was torrid. She would not let him leave until he experienced the true phenomenon that had been happening in our home.

She spun around and screamed, "Show yourself! Show what you can really do! Show him how worthless all of his instruments are! You've been showing us things for months. So show this hack what a haunted house really looks like."

Our home didn't say a word.

Rachel looked around waiting for the worst. She was shaking. Crying. I could see the thoughts racing through her mind. Where is the laughing and clawing? Where are the floating pieces of furniture? Where are the faces that appear in the mirror? Why aren't you here? "Don't play games with me, come on out! I command you to come out!" Rachel screamed again. *This is what a nervous breakdown looks like,* I thought. Dante and I waited silently for a moment, out of respect or even because we were thinking something might actually happen.

Finally Dante said, "I'm sorry we didn't find what you were hoping for, Mrs. Walker." He walked out of our front door and got inside one of the vans. I could see him mouth to one of the drivers, *Let's get out of here.* The vans pulled out of the driveway. I watched them leave and then walked back inside and shut the front door to my completely unhaunted home.

26

Everything Must Go

It was time to leave.

Maybe creatures would follow us, but being here wasn't making things any better. I couldn't wait until the end of the week; couldn't wait for us to find another place or to finish my novel. My wife's sanity couldn't handle being here any longer. I couldn't either, which is why when the ghost hunters left I started to frantically pack things up. I grabbed boxes and armloads of clothes and picture frames and all the junk on our dresser and dumped it into the cardboard boxes. When one box was full, I duct taped it shut and moved on to the next thing. There was no labeling, no system; I just wanted to get everything we owned and pack it away. We'd figure out where everything went later.

Rachel wouldn't help.

She wouldn't really do anything. She lay on the couch, as if affected by some illness, and soaked in daytime television. Every time I tried to talk to her she said something like,

"They think we're lying. They think we're crazy, Charlie. Are we crazy, honey?"

"No, baby. We're not crazy," I said.

"Then why do they think we're lying? Why do they think we're crazy? We're not crazy. We need to give them real proof," Rachel said. Her voice was hollow, distant somehow.

"Honey, maybe their equipment can only sense ghosts. Maybe it can't see demons like we've seen ..."

"You said their equipment should be able to see anything supernatural," Rachel said. She sounded like a child who'd just awakened from a nightmare.

"I know, but, baby, these guys aren't even really experts. It's not like they're doctors or lawyers. They didn't have to go to ghost hunting school. This is far from an exact science. You can't even really prove any of this."

"But they *do* prove things. And we'll find proof. We'll show them. Won't we?" she said. Her eyes were fixed on the TV. It looked a lot more like she was thinking out loud than talking to me. I tried to get her to stop talking like this. I tried to convince her she had to let this go, but she wouldn't listen. She just kept talking about proof again and again; there was nothing else to her. She wouldn't drop this until we left the house.

Which is why I went back to packing. I took our bed-spread and sheets and threw them into trash bags. I took our plates, wrapped them in paper, and stacked them on top of each other.

Late that morning Blake knocked on the door. He was standing there with his hands in his pockets, fending off the Colorado cold, but acting like it wasn't that big of a deal that he was stopping by. It seemed like lately Blake always had something bad and/or awkward to discuss, but he was trying to be cool about it, like the boss that tells you you're going to have to work on Saturday yet still wants you to like him.

"Hey Charlie."

"Hey Blake. Are you on your way to work?"

"Yeah. It's just, I wanted to make sure you guys were okay. I saw a bunch of vans here this morning ..."

"We're fine. Thanks for asking," I said.

I started to shut the front door. But before I could get it all the way closed, Rachel said, "Actually, we're not okay." She'd emerged from upstairs and she looked frightening. Her hair was frazzled and her eyes were yellow and hollow somehow. "They think we're crazy."

"Honey, now is really not the time to talk about this," I told Rachel.

But she kept walking toward Blake. She wanted a new audience to listen to her sermon. "They think nothing's been happening here. But do you know how much we've seen?"

"Rachel, that's enough."

"No, I asked him a question. Do you know how much we've seen?"

"How much what?" Blake asked. He always had this big-brother concerned tone in his voice.

"Creatures, demons, ghosts ... we've seen a lot."

"I believe you," Blake said. He sounded frightened, as if he felt like he might be talking to a creature, demon, or ghost himself.

"But they don't believe us."

"Who doesn't?" Blake asked.

235

"Those ghost hunters. They think we've made it all up," Rachel said.

"You hired ghost hunters?" Blake asked me.

"Rachel wanted validation. This has all been difficult for her."

"It's been difficult for me?"

"Well, hasn't it?"

"Yes, I'm the pathetic victim here, aren't I? Except I know the truth. This house is haunted. You know that too, don't you, Blake?" Rachel asked.

"I don't use words like 'haunted.' If you want my honest opinion, I think there's some real spiritual warfare going on in your house and the only person who can free you from it is Jesus. He's the person who has the truth."

I wasn't sure if Blake meant Jesus would tell us if our house was haunted or not, or if he was referring to a deeper metaphorical or spiritual truth. "You don't need to know if the house is haunted or not. You need God in your life. You need purpose and redemption—"

"Who made you our priest?" Rachel asked.

"No one made me anything ..."

"You put on this face like you have everything together even when your own home isn't in order. You can't even get your wife pregnant ..."

"Rachel," I said. I wasn't sure how she could know that, but I saw Blake's face turn grey and knew she was telling the truth.

"You've tried and tried and tried. You visited specialists and they all say there are a lot of different factors. But you know the truth. Don't you?" My wife's eyes glowed as she told Blake, "It's your fault. You're a pathetic man who can't even—"

"Rachel," I snapped. I turned to Blake. "I'm so sorry. It's been a long day, we didn't sleep last night and ..."

"See you around, Charlie." Blake was in a trance. He stepped away from our porch and slinked back to his home.

I looked at Rachel, but she didn't say anything. She walked back to the couch and turned on the TV. I sat on the edge of the couch next to my wife. "How could you say—"

Rachel cranked up the volume on the TV. She kept staring at it intently and pretending I wasn't even there. I'd gone too far. I hadn't supported her in front of the ghost hunters and now I said she was the one with the problem in front of Blake. And she lashed out at him—

(How did she know that? Did Tammy tell her they were having problems?)

—because of it. I left Rachel and went upstairs and found Adam in his room. "We need to pack everything up. Go get some boxes from the basement and then put whatever you want in them. We're leaving."

"Why, Daddy?" Lucy asked. She'd walked in behind me.

"Remember how I said we're going to live here for just a couple of months?"

"Yeah, Daddy," Lucy said.

"Well those months are over. So go pack your stuff up."

"Okay, Dad," Lucy said and ran to her room.

"Did they find any ghosts?" Adam asked.

"No, they didn't," I said.

"Why not?"

"I don't know, son."

Adam made his way downstairs to get some boxes, but that's when he saw Rachel. "What's wrong with Mom?" he said as he stared at her in the wood-paneled living room lying on the couch and watching TV.

I remembered being around Adam's age and looking at my mother so helpless and lifeless on the couch. I remembered thinking for the first time in my life that I was stronger than my mother; I could run and jump and she could barely move. For my entire life she was the one who helped me: she helped me get dressed, she helped me after a horrible first day of kindergarten, she helped me with homework — but when I looked at her on that couch I realized I had to help her now. The strong mother that I'd grown up with wasn't around anymore. There was only this weak woman on the couch who used all of her energy just to watch TV. I hated realizing that about my mother. I didn't want Adam to look at Rachel in the same way. "Let's leave her alone. She's not feeling very good."

Adam ignored me and made his way over to Rachel. "What's wrong, Mom?"

"They didn't believe us, honey," Rachel said, taking her eyes off the TV.

"Who didn't believe you?"

"The ghost hunters."

"Why not?" Adam asked.

"Because they are small men. They don't understand how ghosts really work. They don't understand what all your father and I have seen. I don't even think your father understands anymore."

"What all have you seen?"

"We've seen creatures, heard noises, we've seen —"

I grabbed Adam's shoulder firmly. "Get boxes. Go up to your room and pack up." He was ready to argue, but I gave him a stern look and he sulked away. I turned to Rachel. "We said we weren't going to talk to the children about this."

"We never said anything. It was all you. You always said everything." Rachel focused her attention back to the TV. Her faced looked pale and her eyes were sunken in—she didn't look like my wife at all—just some distorted version of her. It was this place. This place was stretching her soul thin. We had to leave. But would Rachel even leave this place? She was obsessed and she was turning into—

(Demons don't make us do anything. They just take our weaknesses and exploit them.)

—well, I didn't know what she was turning into.

I couldn't try to analyze this. I just had to keep packing. When we got out of here we could gather ourselves, make sense of things, figure out what to do with our lives next. I checked on Adam and Lucy and they were carefully stacking their toys in cardboard boxes. Folding their clothes and putting them into trash bags. They were both still in elementary school and they were doing a much better job of packing than I was. That was because they still cared about stuff. I no longer cared about our material goods. I could have struck a match to this place and watched the whole thing burn. I just wanted my family to be okay. But there were of course practical matters to consider. We still didn't have a place to live and I didn't have a job, so we needed our stuff.

We spent the rest of the evening, and finally it got so late that Adam and Lucy started tucking themselves in. Rachel had even crept up to our bedroom. We would all sleep.

Morning would bring clarity like it always did. I crawled into bed, exhausted from getting no sleep the night before. Rachel was still awake. I could feel it. I told my wife, "We're leaving tomorrow. We have enough things packed. We'll come back for the rest later. But we're leaving."

The only answer she gave was rolling away and pulling the covers up to her neck. She wouldn't let me see the expression on her face. She wouldn't let me see what she was thinking or if the woman I'd married was even there at all.

* * *

It was an ungodly time of night.

Somewhere between two and four a.m. These are the darkest hours; the time the devil does his worst. It's the time of night where nothing make sense, where you're sleeping so deeply you don't know who or where you are, and the only reason to ever wake up at this time is to stumble into the bathroom or to get a drink because your throat's so dry that you just can't swallow anymore.

I woke up to see Lucy standing next to my bed. She was as quiet and peaceful as the Dali Lama. She didn't shake me awake, she didn't say anything. I looked at her blonde hair and freckled face. Her freckles looked like baby crickets in the moonlight. "Honey, what are you doing? What's the matter?"

"I had another nightscare."

I clicked on the lamp next to my bed. "You did? What happened?"

"The creatures were back."

"Were they crawling all over Mommy?"

"Yes. All over."

I knew it. Ghost hunters could have all of their equipment—the only ghost hunting device I needed was my six-year-old daughter. Of course the creatures hadn't left Rachel alone from that night in the forest. It was clear from the way she'd been acting over the last twenty-four hours. If Lucy dreamt something I could believe it. Which is why I was so horrified by what she said next.

"They were crawling all over Mommy *and* Adam," Lucy said.

My heart sunk. Cold sweat dripped down my face. Was I dreaming this? Was my subconscious creating a dream where Lucy told me my worst fear? Surely, this was just that deep-down voice telling me what I already knew—we had to get out of here.

I pinched myself. I knew that's what you're supposed to do when you're not sure if you're dreaming, but I didn't know people actually did that.

I could feel it. I raked my hands across my face. I could feel that too. And I was thinking that I was dreaming. Isn't that the number one way to know you're *not* dreaming?

"I'm not dreaming this, am I?"

"No, Daddy."

"Rachel, wake up," I said. "I think something's wrong with Adam." I felt over to her side of the bed. There was nothing but comforters and sheets. She wasn't there. "Come on, baby," I told Lucy.

Lucy followed me into Adam's room. I turned on the lights. The room was empty. The boxes were scattered around just like we'd left them before he went to bed. The covers were turned over as if he'd pulled them off to get up in the morning.

"Adam?" I said.

The room didn't say anything back to me.

I turned on the lights in the hallway and I saw more boxes. "Adam? Rachel?" I said.

More silence.

"Where are they, Daddy?"

"I don't know." I couldn't even sugarcoat it to my daughter. I was scared and she could see it.

She followed me downstairs. I turned on the lights in the kitchen, the living room, the dining room, and the den. It was just as we had left it—boxes scattered everywhere. I went to the front door and turned the handle. Locked. It was still locked, thank God. I looked at the windows and they were all still intact. I walked to the sliding glass door and it was still latched shut too. No one forced their way in here.

I opened the front door and looked outside. The car was still parked and everything else in the neighborhood was dark and lifeless. Lights were out in every home. The streetlights weren't even on. "Adam! Rachel!" I screamed. The neighborhood stayed silent.

I shut the door.

That's when I knew exactly where they were. I even knew what they were doing. I couldn't believe it was happening. But it was the only answer that made sense. "Wait here," I told Lucy.

"Daddy, don't leave me," she said.

"Okay," I nodded. "Come here." I picked her up and held her as I opened the door that led into the basement. As soon as I opened the door I could see the candlelight. It was flickering and casting shadows over everything as we crept down the stairs. I could hear whispering. I couldn't tell where or what it was coming from.

When I turned the corner I saw Rachel leaning over the Ouija board with Adam. He had both of his hands on the planchette. My son had his eyes closed and his hands were sliding across the board.

Rule #1: *Never involve Adam and Lucy.*

She had done it. Rachel had done the unthinkable. The other rules, they were all just in place to keep things safe. But there was one rule that was above all others. There was only one rule that really mattered — **Rule #1**, to keep Adam and Lucy safe, to never involve our children in the torment and confusion this had brought us. She hadn't forced Adam to do anything. He was basking in it. His eyes were closed. He took deep breaths and let the evil course through him as it slid his hands across the board. Rachel brought our son down here to baptize him into this darkness.

"What is going on here?" I barked.

Lucy jumped in my arms. Rachel and Adam looked up at me.

"He wanted to know!" Rachel shrieked. "He asked me to show him —"

"You brought him down here?"

"He wanted to see the ghosts. I wanted to show him proof."

"You snuck him down here. You waited until I was asleep to bring him down here . . ."

"You wouldn't understand," Rachel snarled.

"There's nothing *to* understand. These are our children. You can't do this to our children!" I shouted. Lucy covered her ears when I yelled. But she couldn't take her eyes off her brother. Maybe she could see what I saw in the forest: those creatures twisting around Adam. Their yellow eyes glowing. Sniffing. Snarling. Thirsty to gobble his flesh.

"Dad, I just wanted to see the ghosts."

"There are no ghosts, Adam. There were never ghosts. We've never seen a ghost. We've seen a lot of darkness. And all of this has brought us nothing but confusion." I picked the Ouija board up. It was so cheap and flimsy; it was amazing that something like this could bring us so much pain. All I wanted was to take this cheap particle board and tear it in half and then I'd light it on fire and get it out of our life forever.

That's exactly what I did.

I tore that board in two. I took the candle and began to light the edges of it on fire. I walked over to the planchette and stomped on it. I screamed at it as it snapped into pieces. I kept stomping. I wanted to crush the life out of it. Rachel hissed at me. Rachel and I had been in quite a few arguments in our thirteen years of marriage, but hissing was a whole new level for our spats. Then again, this wasn't Rachel. This was some warped, distorted version of her. But Adam and Lucy wouldn't be able to tell the difference. Who knew what else she would do to them if I kept them around her. I told my kids, "Go get in the car." They didn't move. "Now!" I screamed.

They ran upstairs. I started to follow them. Rachel said, "You can't leave."

"I'm not letting you around them anymore," I said.

I was ready to turn and walk away, but that's when Rachel

ran up and clutched her hand around my throat. "You leave now and you'll never see her again." I looked in her eyes. She wasn't there. I saw yellow pupils, anger, fear, and darkness, but I couldn't see my wife in there at all. That glint, the zeal for life that I'd gotten so accustomed to, was completely drained from her eyes.

I pushed the hand off my throat. "I'll be back for her. And until I get back you're not going to do anything at all."

I rushed up the stairs, out the front door, and into the car. I told my kids to buckle up and twisted the key. I looked back up at the house and Rachel was staring at us through the front window. She looked like a ghost. Her eyes were glowing and her head was cocked to the side and I wondered what she was thinking at that moment. Was she even in there at all? Could she tell how twisted she had become? Was there some part in her screaming *This isn't me! That wasn't me that grabbed your throat. Charlie, I love you and I'm so sorry. I didn't mean for this to happen. Please help me, Charlie. Please don't let this happen. Please don't leave. Are you just going to leave like this? After all that we've been through; after all that I've done for you? All those times when you were sick and I brought you chicken noodle soup and Sprite? After our wedding night when I was scared, I wasn't sure about leaving my parents and being with you forever, but you held me and said I had nothing to be afraid of. When you told me you would always hold me and protect me. Is this what you meant by holding me and protecting me? That you would leave me at my darkest hour? Charlie, what are you doing? Get back here.*

You can't just leave like this.

You can't just leave.

You can't . . .

245

I put the car in reverse. I couldn't let myself think like that. If there was some part of her screaming then I couldn't see it. When I looked up she was standing there smiling at me. Her eyes said, *Come back in here. I dare you.* She stood in front of that window and radiated evil. I couldn't even look at her as I pulled out of the driveway, but I could feel that gaze burrowing into me. Whatever that was inside of her wasn't sad I was leaving. It was delighted it had her all to itself.

27

Proof

I forced my eyes open. It was dark but it felt like morning. I wanted it to be morning— I couldn't force myself to sleep anymore. Not that I slept. As soon as I shut my eyes I kept seeing a hand closing around my throat; kept seeing custard eyes; kept hearing that gurgled voice announce, *Leave now and you'll never see her again.* I reached over to feel Rachel. I just wanted to touch her shoulder and know she was okay. She wasn't in bed with me. She was just where I left her, back at the house, staring out the window looking more Bloody Mary than Rachel Walker.

Once I was a little more awake, I realized the room was dark because the blackout curtain made it that way. For the second time in two days I spent the night at the Castle Rock Holiday Inn. I looked across the bed and saw Adam and Lucy. They looked like refugees. We'd all slept in our clothes because when your wife's demon possessed and threatening to kill you and your children, there's no time to think about things like packing an overnight bag.

I rolled out of bed and went to the shower. I don't know how long I stood there. I just kept letting the water run over me, hoping it would make me feel better. I finally pulled myself out of the shower and Adam and Lucy were watching *SpongeBob*. Lucy looked at me and asked, "What's for breakfast?" This was a good question. This was the type of question that I was able to answer in my frazzled state. If she would have asked, Where's Mommy? Why isn't she with us? Why did you just leave her last night? Do you think she's okay? Do you think something happened to her last night? — any of those questions might have made me snap. I may have pulled handfuls of hair out of my head and ran down the street screaming.

But breakfast. I could get us breakfast.

In the lobby the continental breakfast was in full bloom: people everywhere; milk on Fruit Loops; cold cream cheese spread thin across toasted bagels; batter poured on waffle irons; travelers with paper plates searching for a place to eat.

Adam and Lucy went to get some sort of sugary cereal, the type of cereal their mother would have never let them eat had she not been possessed, and I stood in the waffle line. There was a large plastic box with a black spout in front where the batter came out. You then put the batter in a cup and poured it onto the waffle iron. The man in the Hawaiian shirt in front of me grabbed a cup, pulled the spout, and only the smallest amount of batter dribbled out. From the way he sighed you would have thought someone just told him his home was going into foreclosure. Or maybe his daughter just admitted that she'd wrecked his brand-new cherry red Lamborghini. But what you wouldn't have thought was he sighed like that simply because the machine was out of waffle batter. He was completely crushed, as if the only reason he stayed at this Holiday Inn was because of their brand name waffle batter.

I was disgusted at the man in this Hawaiian shirt. His family was perfectly fine. They were probably heading up for a vacation in the beautiful Rocky Mountains. They didn't have cancer and they weren't demon possessed. He had no idea how serious things were all around him. And I wished he could see what things really looked like around him. I wished his guardian angel would drop the scales off his eyes just like Gabriel had dropped the scales off mine. What would this man see if that happened?

He'd reach for the waffle iron and two demons would tug on his arm. They'd get ready to slam down the iron until he had burnt little squares all over his hands and arms; he'd scream that it hurt so bad as skin boiled like waffle batter. Only right before the demons slammed the waffle iron down, his angel would swing down its battle-axe and crush those demons. Their guts would spray all over the wall and slide down it like pulpy orange juice.

I looked all around the lobby. I watched my fellow members of the human race enjoying their breakfasts. Business travelers and families and young couples basking in their budding romance. If only they understood the supernatural battle that was happening everywhere. I pictured the scales falling off everyone's eyes. We'd all see demons run across our tables. They'd slide chairs and write messages with our

Cheerios. They'd scream like lunatic banshees when some-one brought out some Wesson Oil to put on the waffle irons. They'd sniff and snarl and claw and scratch their way inside us. They'd make the upset angry, the angry furious, and the furious stark raving mad. But that's just the beginning.

They'd claw us apart if it wasn't for our guardian angel fighting to keep us sane and bringing us peace, love, and happiness in the process. Our guardian angels, who'd stand on each side of us with flaming swords keeping demonic forces at bay while we sipped on our coffee. God, I wished everyone could see that. Because if we could maybe we'd live our lives differently. Maybe we'd be kinder to our families, gentler to our spouses, and maybe we'd act civil when the plastic box ran out of waffle batter.

I couldn't stand in the waffle line any longer. Besides, I didn't need a waffle. I wasn't hungry. How could I eat when my wife was a prisoner in our own home? When she was an inmate in her own body? I poured myself a plastic cup of orange juice and sat with my kids. They were both hunched over their bowls, scooping fruit-colored cereal into their mouths. Adam had a mouthful of cereal and asked, "Dad, is Mom okay?"

"Yeah, son, she's fine. She just needs a little space."

"How much space does she need? Does she need the whole house to herself?" Lucy asked.

"No, not that kind of space. Well, maybe that too, honey. But she just needed some time alone. You know how when you get really worried about things you feel a little sick and scared? That's how your mommy is right now."

"What's she worried about?" Lucy asked.

"She's worried about the ghosts," Adam answered.

"If I was worried about the ghosts I wouldn't want to be at our scary house all by myself," Lucy said. Like usual, my daughter was right. Rachel shouldn't just be in there by herself. But if I went in there what would she do to me? The way she looked at me it wasn't even her. I could picture running in the door to see her: hair disheveled, eyes yellow, crouched in a corner, and drinking expired milk. She'd look up and charge at me like a puma. She'd pounce on me and claw and bite and try to tear the skin off my face with her fingernails. I couldn't just walk in there.

I needed a plan.

I could call the cops. But they'd just lock her up, throw her into some sort of mental health facility. Her mental health was fine. It was her soul that was in jeopardy. Which is why I needed Gabriel. He could have his all-powerful glowing sword and I'd load up a couple of super soakers with Wesson Cooking Oil. I'd spray down the creatures and they'd melt like the oil was battery acid. We'd kick down the door and wage war on my home and pull my wife from the wreckage.

But Gabriel wasn't around.

Neither was God.

They'd both left me to fend for myself.

I took another drink of orange juice and said, "I've got to make a couple of phone calls." I looked at Adam "Take care of your sister." He nodded yes and then shoveled another spoonful of Fruit Loops into his mouth.

I went outside and took out my phone. The wind was whipping around in gusts and it was bitter cold. The sky was grey. It looked like there was a storm coming. I found a cove in a building where it was quiet enough to have a conversation. I knew I had to be outside because I had to be absolutely sure I was out of earshot of my children. I couldn't let them know just how worried about their mother I was. I stood in the cove and scrolled through my contacts until I found "Dad."

I dialed.

"Hello," Dad said.

"Dad?"

"Charles," he said. He sounded worried. He knew things in the way only a parent can. It was one thing that I called. Another thing that I called this early.

"Hi Dad," I said.

"Son. Are you okay? Is something the matter?"

"It's Rachel."

"What's the matter with Rachel?"

"She's sick," I said. I couldn't bring myself to say "demon possessed." I didn't even know if that was actually the case, and even if it was, how was I supposed to know if he'd believe me?

"Sick," Dad said. I could hear how broken his voice instantly was. He knew about sickness. And I'm sure some time in his life he went into that cathedral, lit a candle, and prayed that I'd never have to face the horror that he faced when he was my age. A wife that was sick and dying, again, that was almost too much for him to bear. I could feel that over the phone. Maybe he would have been better off if I would have just said I think Rachel's demon possessed.

"What's the diagnosis?"

"It's early on, I don't know yet. But it's serious." I was

crying now. God, I was standing outside of the Holiday Inn with the phone pressed against my ear trying to block out the wind. "I don't know what to do, Dad. What did you do when you found out with Mom?"

"I just dropped everything. Things that seemed so important just a few days ago, my career, our finances, whatever, I couldn't even remember why any of that ever mattered. All I could think about was your mother. Doing whatever I could to make her better."

"So what do I do?"

"You fight this."

"I don't know how to."

"Then you find someone that does," my dad said. "You find someone with the cure. And you beg them. You get on your knees and beg. Grovel. Don't let money, but for sure don't let your own pride, get in the way. Don't let this overtake Rachel."

My phone beeped. The cell phone battery was dying. I hadn't charged it after last night. "Dad, I have to go. My phone's dying."

"Okay, Charlie. You protect that family of yours. And you do whatever it takes to save Rachel."

Inside Adam and Lucy were finishing up breakfast. So was everyone else. Things in the lobby were winding down. That meant I needed to leave soon —

(You don't have anywhere to go.)

—but I just needed a plan. Dad was right; I'd beg for help. I'd get on my knees, I'd crawl through glass, I'd sell my soul to save my wife. I thought of Gabriel. *Show up. Just show up here right now. I don't care what you're wearing. You can be in all*

253

white or you can be dressed like a plumber or doctor or an Olympic swimmer. I don't care. I just want you to help me. You don't even have to do anything, just tell me what to do.

I scanned the lobby. There weren't any angels here. None that I could see anyway. Maybe they were all standing around and laughing at me in the supernatural dimension. But they weren't showing up in my dimension to help me. Then I thought of the painting in Blake and Tammy's living room. I thought of Jesus standing there bearded and tranquil holding that fire hose. *I need you. Will you help me? I think you made all that laughing and clawing go away on the night we invited something in our living room. And what did I do to repay you— well, I kept chasing the stuff. So that was a sucky lame way to repay you and honestly I'm sorry. Okay? Blake said you forgive us an infinite number of times, and I've probably used all of that forgiveness up, but I'm still asking you to forgive me now. I'm asking for you to help me save my wife. Show me what to do.*

My eyes were guided toward a table where a mother picked up her toddler. The little girl's face was so green it made her head look like an olive with a red bow for a pimento.

The mother asked, "Are you okay?"

The little girl smiled diabolically before she threw up green baby food all over her mother. And as I watched this happen, for the first time in my adult life I felt that God loved me. And I knew exactly what to do.

I took twenty dollars out of my wallet and handed it to Adam. "Use this to buy lunch. But stay in the hotel until I get back. Don't go anywhere else. I'm going to be back as soon as I can."

"Where are you going?" Adam said.

"I'm going to get your mother," I said. Then my children watched as I ran through the opening of the sliding doors and out of the hotel.

28

Confession Booth

The last time I'd set foot in a Catholic church was when I was seven years old; the night my mother died. Since that day I hadn't set foot in a cathedral, but they were just as I remembered them: stained glass windows depicting events from the Passion Week, wooden pews, a crucifix, paintings of the mother Mary, and tables with candles flickering. I wasn't here for any service, and in fact I didn't know if the church would be open at all.

Luckily, it was. But I needed more than a church, I needed a priest. I looked around the sanctuary and there was no priest inside waiting for me. I half hoped I'd find one inside doing some menial task like cleaning or refilling the holy water, and he would be just waiting for a distressed soul to walk in off the street so he could help with the perfect bit of knowledge and information. This is how it happens in all of the movies.

Like always, movies were false advertising.

There was no priest inside.

I wandered around until I found an office area in the back. The area was old and musty; it looked like it was designed in the 1980s, which made me think of my rental home, which made me think of Rachel, which made me think I had to find a priest right away. I saw a door with a gold nameplate that read "Father Martin" on it. I made my way toward the door until I heard a shrill "May I help you?"

I turned around and saw the receptionist. She looked more like she should be a librarian than a receptionist at a Catholic church. Then again, I knew nothing about what Catholic receptionists look like, so maybe they all looked like librarians. "I need a priest," I told her.

"What for?"

"Because my wife is demon possessed." After a couple of days of nearly no sleep and lots of emotional trauma I didn't have a lot of filters. Besides, my father said to beg and be direct and fight for my wife. And then God made the baby lose its breakfast. Or made me turn in time to see it, anyway. And to a horror writer, seeing a child smile and then release green vomit could only remind him of *The Exorcist*.

I needed an exorcism for my wife.

I had tried praying the prayers of Blake and his prayer team, but those seemed half made up. And what if I was praying them wrong? Priests knew what they were doing. I knew from *The Exorcist* that exorcisms were serious business. It was all about *the ritual* of the thing. All of this demonic stuff was about rituals. There was a ritual just to conduct a séance or play "light as a feather, stiff as a board" or for a game of Bloody Mary. If it took that sort of a ritual just to invite evil in, what would it take to get evil out? So, I needed help, and there was no beating around the bush. I needed to let this receptionist know so she could get on the horn and call 911 to a whole team of priests.

"Your wife is demon possessed?" the receptionist asked.

"Yes."

"How do you know this?"

"Because I saw it happen."

"Where at?"

"At the seventh most haunted place in Colorado."

"Well, I'm sorry, you can't see Father Martin. He's busy."

"Is someone else in there? I'll wait."

"No. He's not here."

"Where is he?"

"Lunch."

"Do you know where he's eating lunch?"

"I'm not allowed to say."

I leaned over the receptionist's desk. She stopped typing on her computer and looked at me. "Listen, I'm sure I sound really crazy right about now. So I wouldn't blame you for not telling me. But I'm only crazy because I'm worried about my wife. She's the mother of my two beautiful children. See, look." I brought up the family picture I had on the home screen of my cell phone. In the picture it was springtime and Adam, Lucy, Rachel, and I were smiling. "See how beautiful and normal and happy she looks? Well that woman doesn't exist right now and I'm very worried about her. And not just her, but her soul. Anywhere else in the world I would think this would sound crazy. But this is church. This is the place where worrying about the fate of someone's soul is no laughing matter. I need my wife back. My kids need their mom back."

The receptionist looked at the picture on my phone and seemed to consider my plea. She turned her glare back to me and said, "He usually eats at Broadway Deli right down the block. He's probably just ordered his Reuben sandwich."

* * *

The deli was full of customers gobbling BLTs, tuna melts, chips, pickles, and potato salad. Most people were in booths catching up with friends or discussing business, but in the back corner was a man in all black with a white collar about to take the first bite of his Reuben. I made my way over to him and sat down across from him uninvited. Rachel was in too much trouble to worry about any formalities.

"I need your help," I said.

He wiped a smudge of Thousand Island off the corner of his mouth. "I don't believe we've met."

"I'm Charlie Walker."

"Father Martin. And I would be happy to help you if you have an appointment. You can make one with my receptionist back at—"

"She's the one who sent me here."

"She did? She knows I don't like to be interrupted at lunch."

"This is urgent."

"I'm sure whatever problem you got yourself into took more than an hour. It can wait until after lunch to be solved." He took a drink of his water and expected that little nugget of wisdom to be enough to scare me off. As if I would say to him, *Wow, I never thought of it like that.* But all it did was tell me I needed to get his attention.

"My wife is demon possessed," I said.

"Really? Wow, I didn't realize I was talking to an expert on the subject. Please, tell me how you know your wife is possessed?" Father Martin was as sarcastic as my guardian angel. Really? All the priests out there and I had to get the sarcastic one.

"Do you want to know the truth?"

"You don't seem very bashful."

I confessed everything: moving, inviting the evil just for the sake of my novel, dabbling and tricking my wife to go along with me. Only now she was consumed by it. I told him what she did last night. I told him how her eyes looked, how she grabbed my throat, how she said *if you leave you'll never get her back.* I told him, "Think whatever you want about me, but wait until you see what's going on in my wife. There's something wrong. Something dark. I mean, have you ever even seen a demon?"

"Yes, I have."

"You have?"

"Yes."

"So, I'm not crazy."

"I don't know you well enough to say if you're crazy or not. What I do know is that I believe in the type of darkness that you're talking about. I've assisted with two exorcisms in my time as a priest. I was young, new to the cloth when I helped out with those, but I saw things there that still haunt me. It's impossible to walk away from an exorcism and to not truly believe in demonic darkness."

"So you'll help me?"

"I might be able to help you," Father Martin said.

"Thank you."

"Once you make an appointment with my receptionist," he said and took another bite of his sandwich.

"I need help now. Today."

"It doesn't just work like that. I can't just say, well, I have an opening at three o'clock so sure, I'll do an exorcism."

"Why not?"

"One, I don't perform exorcisms. Two, there is a process for them to happen. There has to be an investigation and there has to be proof—

(Proof is fool's gold. Is there any way to really prove what had happened?)

—and that's very hard to come by. The church almost never grants exorcisms anymore because of all the medical and legal ramifications to them. So yes, I *might* help you but it takes time. It's a process."

"I don't have time for a process. There is a supernatural battle going on for my wife right now. I need priests, angels, holy water, and crucifixes at my house in the next half hour."

Father Martin took another drink of water. He looked me up and down, probably to size me up, and from that glance he guessed, "You don't belong to a church."

"Why do you say that?"

"Because I'm waiting to hear where you own up to your involvement in all of this. You keep talking about all of these props. Holy water and Ouija boards, and you don't seem to understand God doesn't care all that much about them. We have crucifixes to remind us of God as a tangible piece to a supernatural reality. It's the same with these instruments you've used to get closer to the evil. But it's not about the props. This battle is about your soul. And it's about your wife's soul."

"Yeah, but I've seen things, father. I've seen angels and demons fighting, I've seen the way things really are in the supernatural—"

"There you go again. Talking about angels and demons. As if they're the important things. Yes, they're fighting, but they're fighting over you. Demons exist to attack you; angels to help you. You're the thing God cares about. He cares what happens to you. He cares what happens to your wife. He cares about who you've become."

"What do you mean by that—*Who I've become?*"

"There are only two choices in this world as to the type of person you can be. The first choice is darkness, which means that you do whatever you can for yourself. The second type of person lives with faith, lives selflessly, and makes decisions for others no matter what it costs. I'm still trying to learn to be that sort of person. And I think that's the type of person you can be."

"Great. As soon as I get through this I'll stop everything and *become* a better person," I said.

"You're not listening to me. I'm not telling you to stop doing things. Everyone thinks God is a person who wants you to stop doing bad things—

(This is a waste of time. This priest is not going to help you. He's just going to preach a sermon to you. Did you hear what he's said? It's been years since he's done an exorcism. He doesn't even

know how to fight darkness anymore. All he knows how to do is hide in his office and then come out to eat sandwiches.)

—that's not what the Christian faith is about. Jesus didn't spend his time simply saying *don't* do this, but more importantly faith asks us what we are spending our time *doing*. We are told to lose our life so that we might find it. Maybe if you start doing that you can save your wife."

"You're talking like this is a distant problem. My wife is in serious trouble right now. I need something to happen in her today. I need a miracle in the next twenty-four hours. Not some gradual change in our hearts. And you're telling me that I can save my wife if I start acting better ..."

"What I'm *telling* you, Mr. Walker, is that the problem isn't with your wife at all. Your problem is with you."

"Okay, it's with *me*. What do *I* need to do?"

"You need to start living with faith and you can save her. I mean, you might as well, one way or another it seems you're going to put your faith in something. You had faith that some force was going to move your hands across a board to spell a message. Can't you have the same sort of faith in God for a miracle for your wife?"

He wiped his hands off and stood up to leave. He was just going to leave. Did he think he'd just helped me? By doling out some wisdom? I needed real help. I needed holy water and crucifixes and an exorcist. I shouted, "I've already tried to have faith. I've poured vegetable oil all over my wife!" Father Martin just stared at me. Apparently Catholics don't believe in vegetable oil the way the ministers at Blake's church did.

Then the priest turned around and kept walking away. So I shouted, "My wife is demon possessed and you're just going to let her stay like this?" That's when everything in the restaurant stopped. No one took a bite of potato salad—they just stared at this priest and this crazy man yelling at him.

Father Martin looked at me with compassion and said, "Have faith, Mr. Walker. Change yourself and then look to God to change your wife. I think that will save you both. If it doesn't, you come back and find me. But make an appointment next time."

He turned around and walked out the door, and it took everyone else in the deli a good thirty seconds before they went back to their lunches.

29

Sealed Off

I sat in the car outside the home I'd rented just a few months ago. The home with the 1980s exterior, with the lawn that looked like it was watered with arsenic, with the dead elm tree that would fit perfectly in any cemetery but looked spooky and out of place in a suburban neighborhood. This was the home that my wife was locked in, assuming she hadn't left since last night and assuming she was still—

(*alive*)

—okay. I never noticed how out of place our rental home really looked. Everyone else had these polite little homes with square bushes and adorable white picket fences; then there was our home sticking out like Satan's plaything. This was the type of haunted home legendary in every neighborhood—the home children dare each other to go to and ring the doorbell, but no one ever does because they know if they get too close the home might swallow them whole. If Rachel and I stayed here any longer we'd be equally infamous. The house would drive us stark raving mad. We'd spend all day in our bathrobes and tell anyone who'd listen that there are angels and demons everywhere. They crawl in your bed when you sleep; hover next to you when you drive your car; they're all around you right now, and if you just opened your eyes you would see how things really are.

Or at least I'd say this.

But Rachel still didn't believe there was anything evil crawling inside her, pulling her around like a marionette on strings. I needed to show her. No one else was going to help me. I needed to force her eyes open so she could see how dark things really were.

I stormed to the front door, put my key in the lock, and pushed the door —

It thumped into something. I leaned over the bush and looked in the window. I could see the outline of the couch and love seat shoved in front of it. I went back to the door and rang the bell for three straight minutes; I could hear its faint echo inside. Apparently, demons do not have the same compulsion to answer ringing doorbells like humans do.

I ran around to the back and pulled on the sliding glass door. It wouldn't move. There was a board right next to it. She meant business. She intended to keep me and everyone else out. But I wasn't going to just leave Rachel —

(Could I even call her Rachel anymore? I wondered if the creature crawling around inside her had a name.)

—in there.

And that's when I heard a scream. It came out curdled like Lucy's milk when she left it next to the radiator for a couple days. It was Rachel's scream. The creature knew I was here and it intended to maim, torture, and kill Rachel before I could get to her.

I pulled against the door again. It wouldn't open. I slammed my shoulder against the sliding glass. No way I was going to break through it. I ran to the old tool shed in our backyard and opened the doors as wide as I could. There was no light overhead, but some natural light poured through the door. I scanned the tools: shovel, rake, hammer, screwdrivers, axe.

I picked up the axe.

I lifted it up like I was ready to chop down our Christmas tree, only instead I swung into the glass door. It shattered like a windshield struck by a rock when you're going 70 down the highway. There was a spiderweb of glass where I'd left my mark. I pulled the axe up again and began to slam it into the glass door over and over. Blake rushed outside and saw me. He must have thought I'd gone mad. I had the same thought.

"Charlie, what are you doing?"

I looked up at him. I'm sure my face was pale and my eyes were pulsing red. "I went too far. And now she's screaming in there. Do you think it's killing her?"

Blake didn't even understand the question. "Is Rachel okay? Do you want me to call the cops?"

"Yes. Call them. Call everyone you can," I said. "But I have to get to her now." I picked up my axe again and slammed into the glass. This time it went through. I used the axe to clear all of the glass away.

I stepped through the door. Shards of glass landed on me. A piece sticking out from the door cut my arm open. I bled, but couldn't worry about that. Rachel was screaming up there.

Our house had the stench of sulfur. This is what hell smells like. Hadn't I read that somewhere? Was that in Dante's *Inferno*? That creature wanted it to stink like that so it felt more like home. The house gave me chills like a graveyard. There were boxes all over, some duct taped shut, others full of plates, clothes, and picture frames. I felt like an intruder. Everything inside looked foreign. *I didn't actually leave the house like this*, I thought.

"Rachel!" I shouted. "Rachel, it's me, baby. I've come to rescue you. I'm taking you out of here. I'm your knight in shining armor," I said. I wanted to sound sweet and heroic, but I sounded like I was losing my mind.

"Rachel! I am your husband and I am commanding you to come down here." She didn't answer. There was no light in the house. She'd pinned quilts and blankets in front of the windows. I wondered for a moment if she was hiding in the shadows waiting for me to turn my back so she could strangle me. I gripped my axe, walked into the living room, flicked on the light switch, and nothing happened. I flicked on a switch in the kitchen — nothing. The clocks on the oven and micro-wave were off. There was no sign of life on the coffee maker, the DVD player, or any other piece of electronic equipment.

Rachel's demon had shut off the circuit breaker.

It shut her in and now it wanted her in the dark. "Rachel, please come out here. We have a lot to talk about." I listened for anything — footsteps, a shift, clothes rustling, a woman crawling on the ground. In situations like this I always froze. I always waited for something to happen. But I wasn't going to wait today. My wife needed me—even if she didn't know it. I'd crawl through hell itself and chop up any demon along the way to find her.

I couldn't hear her. But I could feel her. And my feelings told me she was upstairs.

I started to make my way upstairs still clutching onto the axe. I thought about putting it down—

(What are you going to do if she charges at you, Charlie? What if she charges right toward your throat like one of those creatures in the forest? Are you really going to swing this thing? How will you explain this to the police? "She was demon possessed." How do you think that's going to go over, Charlie? How long do you think until they haul you away for a very long time?)

—but I held onto it just in case. I shook as I crept up the stairs. I didn't know if I could face this. I whispered, maybe even prayed under my breath, "Gabriel, are you here? Because if you're really as good at your job as you say you are I need your help. I can't face this creature by myself. Help me out one more time. Please, Gabriel. Please help me because I've gone to everyone else and tried everything and no one's really told me what to do. I don't know what I'm supposed to do right now."

My angel did not appear. Once again God had left me in darkness when I needed him most. I was alone as I made my way toward our bedroom. There were dark blankets in front of our windows just like downstairs. I ripped them down. I opened the blinds and sunlight came flooding in.

That's when I heard clicking and gulping in the bathroom.

I twisted the handle. It was locked. "Rachel. Let me in. Let me in NOW."

Nothing. If she wouldn't let me in, I'd make my own way. I held my axe up and swung it down. It split the door open. I reached it over my head and flung it back at the door. This time I'd split a big enough hole to reach inside. I felt for the handle, unlocked it, and twisted it open.

Rachel was sitting on the floor. She was grinning. There was water all over the floor and her bathrobe was soaking wet. Her hair hung in front of her like strands of tangled wires. She looked up at me. Her face was thin, as if she hadn't eaten in a month. Her skin was so pale I could see her veins, and I looked at her twiggy white hands holding an orange bottle of prescription pills.

"Hi, honey. Where have you been?" Rachel said.

"How many of those did you take?"

"All," Rachel smiled.

I stepped foot in the bathroom and she screamed, "Do not come in here!" She dropped the bottle of pills and picked up an X-Acto knife. She held it to her wrists. "Do not take another step."

I never imagined us in this sort of standoff. Me hovering over my wife, holding an axe, her with a razor blade pressed against her wrists. These are the types of stories you see in the six o'clock news, the types you hope only happen to other people.

"Drop that, Rachel. You're not yourself."

"Neither are you," she said and laughed.

I felt into my pocket for my cell phone. I would call—

It was dead.

Think, Charlie. Are you really going to let this happen?

Are you going to let Rachel die right in front of you on your bathroom floor?

"Let me help you, baby. Please," I was sobbing. I couldn't control myself. I wanted to rip free from my own skin. I stepped forward—

"No," she shrieked. "Stay away. DO. NOT. COME. ANY. CLOSER."

"Why?"

"I want to die alone."

"Rachel, stop this."

"I've lost everything. I've pushed you away, I've lost my Adam and my sweet Lucy, and I lost every one of those things because I really thought I saw something. But I'm just a crazy woman—

(*Demons are attracted to victims like mosquitoes to blood. When they see an opportunity they suck the marrow out of it.*)

—without anything."

I remembered Gabriel's words. This still wasn't Rachel. This creature had polluted her mind. It saw an opportunity to convince her that she'd lost everything and that's exactly what was about to happen.

I was crying. I told her, "You're not crazy. I'm right here to help." I stepped toward her again. She pressed the knife to her wrist so hard it drew blood.

"We were supposed to move here to find happiness. So you could finish your book and we could start out lives together and I ruined it all," Rachel said.

"I don't care about any of that," I said.

"Yes, you do," Rachel snarled. "That's all you've cared about."

I thought about what it looked like to her. Every time she and the kids wanted to get ice cream after dinner but I told her I needed to work. The way I told her that if she had a séance with me it would really help me with the research I needed to write this book. Then she gets excited about all of this and I encourage her. I fed off her to write these chapters and I get ghost-hunting equipment to get more ideas. To create more scenes. To write more chapters. When I finally finish with all of that I just want to stop. I want to wash my hands of it. I didn't really care if we did or didn't see anything; I was just using all of this to create a book. I was inviting darkness into my home, right underneath the room where my innocent children slept, for the sake of plot twists.

She wasn't the creature.

I was.

What if I had this all wrong? What if Rachel wasn't the only one possessed? What if some of my thoughts—

(Stop it, Charlie. What are you doing? You're going to ruin everything.)

—weren't even coming from me? What if they were coming from someone else? I'd never had thoughts like this. Thoughts that interrupted—

(You understand things in a way you never have before.)

—until we moved in here. And this other voice hadn't gotten loud until I started pursuing the darkness. I'd thought the only problem was with Rachel, I thought I'd been walking the straight and narrow, but what if some darkness directed me in here? What was I really planning—

(Burn the place down. That's the only way you'll be free. Strike

a match, light it on fire, and watch it burn. Even if you don't make it out in time at least you'll destroy the evil inside.)

—on doing?

I turned and looked at myself in the mirror. I saw more than a burnt-out writer. My eyes were sunken and dark yellow like a couple of honeycombs. If I looked closely enough, there'd probably be insects swarming around inside them. My face was dark and my skin was white as paste. I barely recognized myself. What had I turned into?

That's when I heard Father Martin's words: *What I'm telling you, Mr. Walker, is that your problem isn't with your wife at all. Your problem is with you.*

I looked at Rachel, slumped on the floor in tears, with barely the strength to hold the X-Acto knife to her wrist. She was dying—

(Maybe you should both just die right here.)

—and her beast of a husband stood over her. What if I was just as possessed as she was? What made me think I was so immune to all of this? Maybe I could hide it a little better, but wasn't it possible I had just as much darkness when she looked into my eyes?

I tried to explain myself, "Rachel, listen—"

Rachel pressed the knife down. "LEAVE, CHARLIE!" More blood was dripping from her wrist.

My head was spinning. There was nothing in here that could save us. Then I heard Father Martin's words: *You had faith that some force was going to move your hands across a board to spell a message. Can't you have the same sort of faith in God for a miracle for your wife?*

I took the words of the priest to heart. I closed my eyes

and prayed. "God, here I am. I'm standing here and my wife is about to die and I have to do something. And there's nothing more that I can do. I'm really at the end of my rope. I know that's probably when people run to you most, but I'm another one of those people. Rachel is here and I can't lose her. And well, you're the only one who can save her. So, please help me. Show me what to do."

For a third time Father Martin's words flashed across my thoughts: *There are only two choices in this world. The first choice is darkness, which means that you do whatever you can for yourself ... or the choice to be the second type of person. The type of person that lives faith, lives selflessly, and makes decisions for others no matter what it costs.*

Father Martin was right. And I knew exactly what I had to do.

I walked out of the bathroom and into the office. I picked up my laptop, the machine that held the only existing copy of *Progressive Evil*, and brought it back into the master bathroom. I put it into the sink. "This has gone on long enough," I said.

Rachel leaned forward. She knew what was represented in the laptop. "What are you doing?" she asked. Her eyes were getting milky. She needed help and soon. I hoped Blake had called the police.

"I've acted like this is the only thing that matters. And now I need to show you it doesn't matter at all. None of this matters, Rachel. We can still be saved." I was crying and shaking. I put my hand on the faucet. I thought about all the hours I sat there typing away at another new chapter and discovering one twist after another. I thought I really had something with this book. I was so sure of it I could imagine the book sitting on the front table at Barnes and Noble, I could picture all of the rave reviews, I even knew what actors I wanted for the inevitable movie version. I'd put so much into this. I'd poured my soul onto these pages. No, I'd *sold* my soul to create these pages.

Now I was about to destroy the book to save Rachel.

It was an easy decision. I'd spend an eternity in purgatory creating bestsellers and destroying them if it meant my wife would be okay.

I twisted the knob on the faucet. Water poured all over my laptop with steady innocent whooshing sounds, cleansing my laptop of any knowledge it ever had of *Progressive Evil.* I'd become so obsessed with writing it I didn't know when the last time I backed it up was. Two months ago? Three months? It was tough to say, but I knew it was long enough to destroy everything. I'd never go back and rewrite it. How could I without re-creating all the séances and ghost hunting late into the night?

This book had to die.

I'm not saying this is always how God works. I'm not an expert on that. I'm just saying there was no way for us to be free while that thing still existed. I'm saying for Rachel, I had to show her that I was willing to take a leap of faith. That everything could be okay again. And I think she understood what I was doing. How I was killing myself to save her.

To save us both.

She watched the water rush out of the faucet and all over the laptop and tears streaked down her face. I'd be lying if I didn't tell you about the war waging inside me. The back of my mind or that voice told me there was another way. It screamed at me. But I pushed it away. I took my eyes off my laptop and turned all my attention to my wife. She looked at me. I gave her a look that said everything words couldn't express. That I loved her with every part of my soul. It looked like a little bit of color had come back into her skin and the Rachel I knew and loved and needed returned to her eyes. The X-Acto knife slid out of her hands and she slumped against the wall.

I ran over to her.

I held her.

Water poured over my laptop and my novel as I picked my wife up and carried her downstairs. I needed to take Rachel outside, but my arms were so weak. I placed her on the couch and that's when I could hear it.

Sweet sirens rushing to our rescue. I looked behind the quilt and stared out the window. That's when I saw the cavalry rushing toward us — an ambulance, a fire truck, and police cars. Who knows what Blake told them to get this sort of reception, but whatever he said I was grateful to him for it.

I looked at Rachel. "You stay awake, honey. You keep breathing. Do not fall asleep, baby. Help is coming. Help is almost here." It was too dark in here. I couldn't even tell if her eyes were open or not. I grabbed the giant vanilla cupcake housewarming candle and then some matches from inside one of our end tables. I struck the match and lit the candle so I could see Rachel's face. Her eyes were still open, but it looked like the life was draining out of them. Any second now the firemen would break down our doors. I could picture them rushing in, grabbing her, and putting her in an ambulance where the healing would begin. She'd be driven to the hospital and doctors would do whatever it took.

Any moment they would break down the doors.

Any moment now.

I waited.

And for the second time in my life I stared at a flickering candle while I prayed for God to keep the woman who I loved more than anything else in the world from dying.

30

Spirit Recovery

Six Months Later

Rachel and I walked into a room with metal folding chairs, a white board, and a table with refreshments. Overhead were white fluorescent lights that constantly whined, annoyed they had to go through all the trouble of lighting up the room. Rachel found us a seat and I walked over to the refreshments table. And just to be clear, by refreshments, I mean Chips Ahoy cookies and stale cold coffee. I poured myself a cup of coffee into a Styrofoam cup and topped it off with powdered creamer.

I took a drink.

I'd never had such amazing tasting bitter cold coffee in all of my life. Not that it was the coffee that was good necessarily. It was being here in the spirit recovery class with Rachel. It meant we had survived. It meant we could tell our story. It meant we were alive and I understood now that every day was a gift for both of us.

We started coming six months ago.

It was about a week after I broke down our door and the ambulance rushed Rachel to the hospital. She had to have her stomach pumped; it wasn't pretty, but with demons nothing ever is very pretty in the end. When it was all over the doctor came into our room and said, "Your wife is going to be just fine. Medically speaking anyway. But there are still some questions you'll have to answer to the state workers."

They declared Rachel's case a suicide attempt.

She had to do a week of mandatory therapy in the local clinic. She had to sleep there every night—it was humiliating, depressing, and as she said, "Completely necessary." It was a time of demonic detox for both of us. During that week we also had different ministers pray for any demons/demonic residue to leave us. There was never this dramatic moment where we spit green bile or twitched or snarled. I always felt better after the prayers, but truthfully, I think any demons left us the moment I turned to God and turned the faucet on *Progressive Evil*. I think from that moment forward we were free of darkness. Still, we needed time to get away and process and look at things more clearly.

This meant lots of sessions of counseling. There were times when Rachel talked with counselors, times when I talked with counselors, and lots of times when we talked with each other. It was in those times that we pieced together the story and made sense of everything that had happened in those five months.

But did things just go away that easy?

No, I guess we were like people detoxing from any other vice. Drug addicts get the shakes, alcoholics get thirsty, and as for me, every time I saw something out of the corner of my eye or heard something that didn't quite seem right I'd perk up. I'd imagine it could be the supernatural and I'd want to investigate and that's when I'd stop myself. I'd remember to walk away — I'd remember the prayers Father Martin and Blake have taught me since.

The counselors helped me look at the world differently. I guess they helped both of us get back to normal. They said it was like germs. When someone who suffers from obsessive-compulsive disorder learns about germs they get a Howard Hughes-like fear of the things and imagine them on door handles, public toilets; they can picture them crawling all over food at five-star restaurants. Yes, the germs are there. But you just have to be a little careful. Sanitize your hands now and again. Use a toilet seat cover. You can be smart and safe and careful, but without letting the fear paralyze you.

That's how it is with demons and angels for me. I know they're out there, I know there are things happening all around me I'll never see and never understand. I can't let that paralyze me. I can't assume every time I have a bad thought it's from the devil. I can't assume every time I slow down for a yellow light it's my angel making me tap my brakes to save me from an accident. I'm not saying those things don't happen. In fact, in the opinion of this novelist without a novel, those things happen all the time. But I'll never know when. I've never seen into the other side of things like I did that night in the forest. So instead I look forward.

And honestly, what's helped me look ahead is looking back and writing everything down. This book started as an assignment a counselor gave us. She said, "Why don't you quickly jot down your versions of the story?" Rachel's was two pages.

My version was fifteen typed pages, single-spaced. Once I started writing about this, it poured. The method writer within me is alive and well.

Uh oh, you might be thinking.

Does this mean Charlie Walker hasn't learned his lesson?

I can see why you'd think that. But this time it's different. Maybe all writing is method writing and it's not *how* we write that matters but *why*. You see, somewhere along the way I forgot what writing was supposed to do. Yes, fear inspired the very first successful short story I ever wrote in high school (my only published story to date). But with that story I wasn't writing because of the fear, I was writing to overcome the fear, to move past everything that happened with Mom.

The writing was there to heal me.

And it did heal me for years until I moved my family, bought the Ouija board, and ... well, no need to relive all of that again. All I'm saying is when writing works best, it's there for pure reasons. I forgot that somewhere along the way (probably somewhere near page one) while working on *Progressive Evil*. I didn't want to do that with this story. Truthfully, I wrote our story for pure reasons and I never intended to do anything with it. But Rachel loved it so much she sent it to a publisher that loved it.* They said haunted house stories were "hot" and wanted to publish mine.

I wasn't trying to write anything "hot." I told Rachel,

---

*In case you're wondering, this never happens. Publishers don't read stories and just "love" them. But somehow in my case, it fell into just the right acquisition editor's hands at just the right time. This is another sign that makes me think maybe miracles do happen.

"I can't believe you sent my counseling exercise off to a publisher."

"It's a little more than a counseling exercise. It's a couple of hundred pages now."

"I got a little carried away."

"Well, it's good and it's funny and it's weird and it's honest and I thought other people should read it," she said.

"But there's really personal stuff about us in there."

She said, "I know, but it's all true, and I don't have anything to hide. We survived this, we're better people because of it, and if someone else can learn from us, then maybe that makes everything worth it."

"What about Adam and Lucy? They're in this story too," I said.

"Adam will think it's cool that his name is in the book. And Lucy is wise beyond her years. She'll understand. I think she'll want to help others just like I do."

"But Rachel. There's Blake and Tammy. There's real people in here."

"Well, change everyone's names then."

"Okay," I said. "Let's publish our story." I hugged Rachel and we laughed and we cried at the irony.

We went to more counseling individually and then we started going to a counseling class for people who were recovering from suicide. It was held at a local church. That class didn't really work for us, but then we found another one called The Spirit Recovery class. Every week we sat in a circle and talked about encounters with the supernatural and how to recover from them. We sipped coffee from Styrofoam cups and nibbled on stale chocolate chip cookies among friends who truly understood what it meant to encounter the darkness.

There was a new kid there tonight. He was in his twenties and we all listened as he said, "I just went to get my fortune read. I didn't think it would be that big of a deal."

"No one ever does," I said. Everyone chuckled. It was an understanding laugh that said "We've all been there."

After class we'd always gather around and pray for each other. I believe in prayer now and I'm trying to understand God better, though in many ways that seems to be a bigger and more complex journey than understanding Satan. But I'm up for it. I think I'm even going to take my family to this church on Sunday.

My family.

You might want to know what happened to us. Well, we moved to a new house and have experienced exactly zero haunting incidents in five months. Lucy no longer has nightscares. And I'm going to start teaching English at a new high school this fall. I'm looking forward to the creative writing class. I think I'll have lots more to say this time around.

Author's Note

I have this suspicion that there's a bit of a method writer in all of us. I know there's a method writer alive and well in me. I pull things from my life, turn them into fiction, which then turns them into truth. The grand, important, universal truth with a capital *T* and not the truth associated with facts.

However, I should quickly say that my wife is the least demon-possessed person I know. I would rank everyone else I know from most demon possessed to least demon possessed, but that would take far too much time.

I also want to say if it takes a village to raise a child, it takes a small town to write a book. The people in the town of *Homemade Haunting* are Andy Meisenheimer, advocate, cheerleader, and best friend to all the writing of Rob Stennett; the "Noveldoctor," Stephen Parolini, whose wisdom and insight pushed me to perform much needed editorial surgery on the novel; the good people at Zondervan who have been so flexible and supportive since the word *Go*; and Mike Salisbury, who "got me" and understood the vision of the story and what a cover for a book like this should look like.

Finally, I'd like to thank my daughter Claire for being such a spark as I wrote this. She's a year and a half old and chock full of life and intelligence. Her sister's name was on the back cover of my first book, so I wanted to make sure Claire got her name in print somewhere. So here it is, Claire. You're probably 25 and reading this and it's right before you're getting married (though I'm fine if you don't get married until you're closer to 45. You can even become a nun if you want). Well, congratulations, honey. I hope whoever he is, he makes you as happy as your mother has made me.

Author Q & A

After reading this book, you might have a few chills. And a few questions. Rob was kind enough to sit down with us and answer a few them.

Zondervan: So no one in your family is demon possessed?

ROB: I thought my sister might have been when I was a teenager, but I later learned that a lot of teenage girls act demon possessed.

Z: Well, good to clear things up about your family. Okay, we'd better keep moving. If the idea for this book didn't come from personal experience, where did it come from?

ROB: Originally this book came from meeting someone who told me all about how he used to be heavily involved in the occult, but when he had a family he didn't want to expose them to any of that. I started writing that story; it was actually called *Fallen World*, but I ran into a lot of problems with it. So I thought, What if I flipped it on its head? What if someone with an established family life tried to bring the occult into his home?

Z: *I'd think flipping it around like that would really change the whole story. Not just the plot but what the story was about.*

ROB: Absolutely. Originally the character had more innocence in a way because he was trying to get free from something. It was like this guy told me: It's hard to be a Satanist and a good father. I thought that made sense and it sounded like a fascinating character. But Charlie was guilty of inviting something into his home for the sake of his own career. So for me this story was personal in that way, not really because he was a writer, but because my biggest fear has always been doing some sort of wrongdoing that would affect my wife and my kids. It's the last thing I'd ever want to do. To me, hurting your family in that way is what real life horror is.

Z: *Wow. I didn't expect that answer.*

ROB: I don't think that was the answer I expected to give either. Funny the stuff you come up with when you have questions coming your way.

Z: *Well, let's keep the questions coming and see what else you come up with. This book is funny in moments you wouldn't necessarily expect comedy. Why do you use humor in a story like this?*

ROB: I wanted this story to be in a sort of hyper reality. I think most of my stories are like that. Because those are the stories I love to read. I love authors like Kurt Vonnegut and

Mark Twain who are really funny in one moment and chilling in the next. I think if I were trying to use a Ouija board to get story ideas, it'd be both funny because I wouldn't know what I was doing, and just as scary because I wouldn't know the consequences of what I was doing.

Z: How much of Rob Stennett is in Charlie Walker?

ROB: Obviously the story comes from me, but my life is not nearly as interesting as Charlie's. I would never just quit my job, nor would I keep pushing on something when it seemed so wrong. I'm not nearly as judgmental as he is either. But I do think I rationalize things, so when Charlie made the *5 Rules about Ghost Hunting* I could see myself doing something like that to ease my guilt.

Z: How about any characters or scenes you wanted to write that didn't make the cut?

ROB: I had this scene where I wanted Charlie and Rachel to end up at a progressive dinner in a creepy home like the one Charlie is talking about, but it didn't make sense for the story. I just thought it'd be fun to write.

Z: What's next for Rob Stennett?

ROB: Right now I'm working on potentially developing one of my books into a feature film. It's still in the early phases, but I'd love to see it happen.

Z: Wow, that would be great! Keep us in the loop on that one, okay?

ROB: Absolutely!

Z: Well, Rob, thanks for taking the time to chat with us today and letting us gain insight into the author behind Homemade Haunting. *And for those of you out there with more questions for Rob, drop him a line at robstennett.com. Rob, that's okay that I gave them your contact information, right?*

ROB: For Sure. Keep the scary questions coming.

Discussion Questions
for Homemade Haunting

1. Have you ever taken a risk and moved to a new place in order to pursue a new opportunity? How did you decide between staying in the status quo and pursuing a dream?

2. Charlie's views about God were shaped early in his life. Do you think he would have approached the supernatural differently if he didn't lose his mother as a child?

3. Who holds more of the blame for the haunting at 1282 Voorhees Lane? Charlie or Rachel?

3. Do you think Blake and Tammy were helpful to the Walkers? Should they have interfered more or less?

5. What effect did Adam and Lucy have on their parents? How do you think this story would have turned out if Charlie and Rachel didn't have any children?

6. What do you think kept drawing Charlie and Rachel
   back to pursuing the supernatural even when there was
   obviously a problem?

7. Do you believe in ghosts? Demons? Do you believe
   there's a difference between the two?

The Almost True Story of Ryan Fisher

A Novel

Rob Stennett

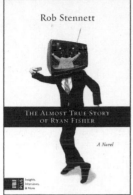

Meet Ryan Fisher—a self-assured real estate agent who's looking for an edge in the market.

While watching a news special late one night, he sees evangelical Christians raising their hands in worship. It's like they're begging for affordable but classy starter homes.

Ryan discovers the Christian business directory and places an ad complete with a Jesus fish. His business doubles in a week.

But after visiting an actual church, Ryan realizes that with his business savvy, he could not only plant a church—he could create an empire.

The Almost True Story of Ryan Fisher is a hilarious, spot-on, and often heartbreaking satire in the tradition of Kurt Vonnegut, Tom Perrotta, and Douglas Adams.

The End Is Now

A Novel

Rob Stennett

One week from tomorrow, at precisely 6:11 in the morning, the rapture or apocalypse or Armageddon or whatever else it is you'd prefer to call it, is going to occur. But only in Goodland, Kansas.

Stuck in the middle is the Henderson family: Jeff, a struggling salesman who lives with a nagging fear that something will happen to his family; Will, who's just trying to figure out life in the fifth grade; Emily, whose greatest concern is that she won't be nominated homecoming queen; and Amy, who is growing stir-crazy from being a housewife for eighteen years — and is convinced this was God's plan B for her life.

The Hendersons are longtime residents of Goodland, Kansas, a small Midwest town where nothing new or exciting ever happens ... until now. Are the recent happenings and catastrophic weather mere coincidence, or more? The town spirals into chaos and confusion as its residents discover the end is no longer near — the end is now.

Rob Stennett's second novel is both a satire and a story of the apocalypse, a thriller and an exploration of family, community, belief, unbelief, and the two-thousand-year-old Christian tradition of looking to the sky because the end is near.

Available in stores and online!

Share Your Thoughts

With the Author: Your comments will be forwarded to the author when you send them to *zauthor@zondervan.com*.

With Zondervan: Submit your review of this book by writing to *zreview@zondervan.com*.

Free Online Resources at
www.zondervan.com

Zondervan AuthorTracker: Be notified whenever your favorite authors publish new books, go on tour, or post an update about what's happening in their lives at www.zondervan.com/authortracker.

Daily Bible Verses and Devotions: Enrich your life with daily Bible verses or devotions that help you start every morning focused on God. Visit www.zondervan.com/newsletters.

Free Email Publications: Sign up for newsletters on Christian living, academic resources, church ministry, fiction, children's resources, and more. Visit www.zondervan.com/newsletters.

Zondervan Bible Search: Find and compare Bible passages in a variety of translations at www.zondervanbiblesearch.com.

Other Benefits: Register yourself to receive online benefits like coupons and special offers, or to participate in research.

ZONDERVAN®

ZONDERVAN.com/
AUTHORTRACKER
follow your favorite authors